Christmas North and South

Two hospitals, four very merry matches...

Great Southern Hospital in London and
Great Northern Hospital in Edinburgh are very special
places. Their close working relationship allows them to
share their considerable talents
and world-class knowledge, from transplant
and reconstructive surgery to neurosurgery and
cutting-edge cancer research. As the festive season
begins, and the sparkle of fairy lights fills the hospital
gardens, staff will be saving lives—and falling in love!

Immerse yourself in the warmth and romance
of the season with...

Tamsin and Max's story
Festive Fling with the Surgeon by Karin Baine

Lauren and Oliver's story
A Mistletoe Marriage Reunion by Louisa Heaton

Both available now!

Skye and Jay's story
Melting Dr. Grumpy's Frozen Heart by Scarlet Wilson

Poppy and Dylan's story
Neurosurgeon's IVF Mix-Up Miracle by Annie Claydon

Coming soon!

Dear Reader,

I always look forward to writing a continuity and wait with bated breath to find out which story I'd been assigned to write. When I discovered this time that I'd been assigned Lauren and Oliver's story, I was delighted and excited to write a story that featured older characters.

I'd not written a romance for characters who were in their fifties before, and being in my fifties myself (ahem!), I wondered, Why not? This was so my jam! And so I had great fun bringing Oliver to life with his regrets over the past, and empathized totally with Lauren, who'd sacrificed her own career to concentrate on her family first. Writing the relationship they had with their grown-up children, Willow and Kayleigh, was a great thing to explore, too.

I really hope you enjoy their story and your time at the Great Southern Hospital!

Warmest wishes,

Louisa x

A MISTLETOE
MARRIAGE REUNION

LOUISA HEATON

MEDICAL ROMANCE

Special thanks and acknowledgment are given to Louisa Heaton for her contribution to the Christmas North and South miniseries.

H Harlequin®
MEDICAL
ROMANCE

Recycling programs
for this product may
not exist in your area.

ISBN-13: 978-1-335-94263-0

A Mistletoe Marriage Reunion

Copyright © 2024 by Harlequin Enterprises ULC

Harlequin Enterprises ULC
22 Adelaide St. West, 41st Floor
Toronto, Ontario M5H 4E3, Canada
www.Harlequin.com

Printed in U.S.A.

Louisa Heaton lives on Hayling Island, Hampshire, with her husband, four children and a small zoo. She has worked in various roles in the health industry—most recently four years as a community first responder, answering emergency calls. When not writing, Louisa enjoys other creative pursuits, including reading, quilting and patchwork—usually instead of the things she *ought* to be doing!

For Jamie, who asked!

**Praise for
Louisa Heaton**

"Another enjoyable medical romance from Louisa Heaton
with the drama coming courtesy of life on a busy maternity
ward. Lovely characters, a great story, set in one of my
favourite cities and an all round easy engaging read."
—*Goodreads* on *Miracle Twins for the Midwife*

CHAPTER ONE

AN AIR AMBULANCE helicopter was coming in to land on the roof of the Great Southern Hospital as Dr Lauren Shaw stood before the entrance in the early-morning dark and cold, trying to work up the courage to step inside.

It was impossible from where she stood to feel the downdraught of the whizzing rotor blades that chopped through the air high above, but it felt that way as a chill breeze tried to blow her blonde hair out of its tight ponytail and she shivered violently, huddling up tighter in her winter coat.

I don't need to be this scared.

It's ridiculous!

I'm a grown-ass woman, for crying out loud!

Oliver wasn't even in the building. Not yet anyway, because Lauren had arrived extra early so she could be ready for anything, figuring that if she were in the hospital first she could establish her ground, get a feel for everything, start to make friends, before he arrived and then, when he did, it would feel like equal territory. Or as equal as she could make it, considering he'd been working here since he qualified all those many years ago.

Who am I kidding?

She knew who he was around here. He was a maxillofacial reconstructive *god*. People came from all over the country to be treated by him, and she knew of his successes because she heard all about him from their daughters, Kayley and Willow, whenever they chatted on the phone, or on her occasional visits. Visits that were always perfectly orchestrated to make sure that Lauren never ran into him.

She'd come down from Edinburgh when Kayley had passed her bar exam and qualified as a lawyer. She'd come down when Willow had qualified as a paediatrician, and taken both her daughters out for a celebratory meal. It had always been a struggle to leave them again and get back on the train to Scotland. And now she wouldn't have to. She was here to stay. Though she'd hoped to *not* get a job at the Great Southern but at another London hospital, when the job for a reconstructive surgeon had come up here her colleagues at the Great Northern had encouraged her to go for the role, telling her how good it would be for her career, the professional move she'd been looking for.

And she and Oliver were adults, right? Surely they could be mature about this. Old feelings, old resentments, old *guilts*, could no longer trip them up, right?

Lauren sucked in a breath.

A journey of a thousand miles begins with a single step. I took that step when I applied for this post.

She stepped forward, eyes focused on the fairy lights that were already up in readiness for the festive season, trying to focus on the beauty of them, how they looked like little snowflakes. The reception area was large, with an L-shaped desk and two receptionists sitting behind it. One was on the phone, the other was handing a piece of pink paper over to a couple of guys. The one facing her was an attractive younger man with thick, dark hair. He was laughing and had a broad, beautiful smile and the other was... The other man was...

Lauren's steps slowed. Something about the man looked familiar. The height, the stance. It couldn't be, could it?

His shoulders were just as wide, just as broad, but his frame was trimmer, more streamlined, the love handles she'd once joked with him about, teased him about even though she'd once loved them, were gone. His hair, that had once been dark and devilish, was now peppered with silver and looked distinguished and sexy in a new style and she had no doubt that those gorgeous green eyes of his were exactly the same!

Dr Oliver Shaw was here early.

Her plan to establish her ground had already faltered.

Her position of power was gone.

All she could hope for now was that she would come across as calm and composed and looking as amazing as he did! The years had been kind to Oliver, clearly. And both Kayley and Willow had commented in the last few years how their dad had got into fitness, went to the gym regularly and had even run in marathons the last few years. No doubt due to the influence of Daria, his much younger girlfriend.

Would *he* think that *she* had changed? That the years had been kind to her? She did yoga now and could do a crow pose easily but, unlike Oliver, Lauren had had to deal with the menopause over the last few years and the silver in her blonde hair was hidden with carefully applied highlights, her own love handles caged in by clever undergarments, and the last time she'd run for anything had been when she'd run away from Mike…

You know what? It doesn't matter what I look like. I'm a strong, confident woman and I'm here to do an excellent job and that's what matters.

*I love who I am and what I look like now. I've
grown into this body and it's beautiful and the
battle scars tell my story.*

It didn't matter what Oliver's opinion of her
might be. Because *his* opinion was none of her
business!

And so she confidently stepped forward to
say hello.

'So you think we can discharge her tomorrow?'
asked Dev.

'I don't see why not. She's been on the antibi-
otics for three days now and hasn't sparked any
more fevers, so I'd say we have a handle on her
infection. Let's continue to monitor her today,
check her stitches tonight and if all looks A-okay
then we can send her home.' Dr Oliver Shaw
turned to Rebecca on reception. 'Bex, were you
able to get hold of that taxi service for me?'

Bex smiled at him, the way she always did,
and handed him a piece of pink paper. It had a
telephone number on it. 'Sure did.'

'Thanks.' He needed it for his patient. She
lived outside of London. She'd come all the way
from Canterbury to be seen by him and have her
upper jaw realigned and he'd promised he'd find
her a decent taxi firm that would get her home
again safely without charging her the earth.

His surgery on Stella Malcolm had gone well,

but her temperature post-surgery had been fluctuating and they'd discovered that she'd had a urine infection, of all things, that had gone into her kidneys. It had made her quite unwell, to the point that she'd begun to hallucinate, but things had calmed down the last couple of days and she seemed back to normal. He'd stayed all night to make sure she was okay, monitoring her, even though his registrar, Dev, had offered to do so. Besides, he'd known he wouldn't sleep well, knowing that Lauren, his ex-wife, was coming back at some point today. To work here, at Great Southern. It just seemed easier to stay up all night and focus on his patient, rather than stay up all night and think about his ex. A good distraction technique.

The last ten years, the Great Southern Hospital in London had been *his* territory. The Great Northern Hospital, its sister hospital in Scotland, had been Lauren's. When he'd heard she was coming back, had applied for the vacancy of reconstructive surgeon, he'd been shocked. Kayley and Willow had both mentioned that their mum had begun to wish to be closer to them again, but he'd never imagined she would come *here!* He'd thought she'd go to Guys and St Thomas' or someplace like that. He'd never imagined that she would want to walk the same halls as him...

And what about her boyfriend, Mike? Had he come back with her? He was a hotshot reconstructive surgeon, by all accounts. Where was *he* working, because it certainly wasn't here!

Oliver noticed that Dev's attention had been caught by someone behind them and so he turned to look, doing a double take when he realised who it was.

Lauren.

Wow, she looked fine! The years had been more than kind. How could she look better than she had before? It had been ten years since he'd last seen her, walking away from him with her bags packed, struggling to carry them all, because she was so small and there'd almost been nothing to her.

He used to call her 'Baby Bird' affectionately, because her five foot three to his six-foot height had made her seem that way. But now? She'd filled out some, had knockout womanly curves. Her face, once so angular, now had perfect cheekbones and her make-up looked different. Whatever she was doing now really made her light blue eyes stand out. They were almost hypnotising. They were—

'Oliver?'

He was vaguely aware that Dev was trying to talk to him, that his friend and colleague was smiling, puzzled, trying to work out why he—

normally so garrulous—had been struck dumb by a hot blonde entering Reception.

She wore heels that accentuated perfect calf muscles. Had she been working out? And now, as she got closer, the fairy lights surrounding the reception desk began to flicker across her face and her eyes gleamed as she stretched out a hand to say hello.

'*Oliver.*'

Speak. You need to speak.

Of course he'd known she was doing all right for herself. Their two daughters had kept him abreast of all their mum's news and he'd been delighted that she had finally been able to throw herself into the career that she'd wanted. But he had to remind himself that she was with Mike now and that today had to be a big change for her too and the last thing she'd need was her ex-husband being struck dumb at the sight of her. She needed him to act normally and in control. To be focused, the way he was when he was in Theatre.

Get a grip.

'Lauren. You're here early.' He somehow managed to dredge up a passable genuine smile and reached out to shake her hand. As soon as he touched her he felt electrocuted, zaps of lightning shooting up his arm that were most troubling. Most disturbing.

Most surprising.

'I wanted to get an early start...you know how it is.'

Her beaming smile when she directed it towards him was awe-inducing in the extreme. It brought everything back. Everything. Why was he reacting this way? Mentally, he tried to get a hold of himself, to find that control he needed if he and Lauren were to carefully navigate this new working relationship. He was a maxillofacial reconstructive surgeon; she was a reconstructive surgeon. They were going to be working together.

'Of course. Lauren, let me introduce you to Dr Dev Singh, one of our highly skilled registrars.'

She shook Dev's hand. 'Pleased to meet you.'

'Pleasure is all mine. I've heard a lot about you.'

'Oh?' She looked at Oliver, but he looked blank because he'd not told anyone anything about her.

'I'm good friends with your daughter Willow. We've worked together on a couple of occasions in Paeds.'

'Ah, yes, I remember her mentioning you. You're the doctor that likes to go rowing, is that right?'

Dev nodded. 'From my Cambridge days.' He smiled.

Oliver stood there, surprised. How had he never heard that Dev liked to row? 'Well…now that introductions are over, should I escort you upstairs? Show you around? Introduce you to everyone?'

Her gaze turned back on him and it was mesmerising. 'Unless there's work that needs doing first? I'm ready to get stuck in.'

Of course. She'd waited long enough to properly focus on her career and he'd played a part in that. Introductions could wait.

'The next patient on my list this morning requires a radial forearm flap for tongue cancer. You could join me on that.'

Lauren nodded. 'I'd love to. Why don't you tell me more about the patient?'

Her smile was bewildering and it hit him in the solar plexus so hard, he almost felt winded.

CHAPTER TWO

'TILLY? THIS IS Dr Lauren Shaw. She's going to be assisting me with your surgery this morning.'

Tilly Garson was a woman of Lauren's age, mid-fifties, who had taken a different route to Lauren and allowed her grey hair to grow through unimpeded. She looked quite stylish with it and was clearly a woman who took care of her appearance. And though Tilly's grey hair suited her perfectly, Lauren wasn't sure she was ready for that just yet.

Tilly looked up at her in surprise. 'Dr *Shaw?* Are you related?'

Lauren smiled politely. She didn't normally like to give out personal details to patients, but she'd never been asked this before, having worked at a completely different hospital to her ex-husband. It had never been an issue. Nor had she ever changed her surname back to her maiden name of Taylor, because she'd wanted to keep the same name as her children. Was this going to be an issue now?

'Er...'

'No. No relation,' said Oliver, jumping in to rescue her.

She turned to look at him, but he didn't meet her gaze. She had not needed rescuing! She would have got an answer out eventually. She'd just needed another millisecond to think of something, some polite way of saying that they were divorced. Was there a way?

But Oliver had got there first and made it quite clear that they were not related. They weren't any more anyway, that was the truth. They just shared a surname. And two children. And a couple of decades of married life.

But nothing now.

And that was good, right? Because he was not hers any more, and though she'd been surprised at her immediate visceral reaction to how he looked—distinguished, sexy, silver fox—his statement made it clear that there was nothing between them *any more*.

Which was perfect, because she didn't want to get involved with Oliver again, except as colleagues who happened to work in the same department. He was senior to her and technically her boss, but that was the only say he would have in her life from this point on. She would prove to him how capable she was. How professional. That was all.

'Tilly, do you have any questions before we go down into Theatre?' Oliver asked.

The patient nodded. 'Yes. I know I said I didn't want to know any of the details before, but I've thought about it and wondered if you might tell me some right now. It's just I figured I could then picture it in my head and visualise good things and send myself some healing thoughts.'

Oliver nodded. 'Of course. Dr Shaw, why don't you explain to the patient what we're doing today?'

He was testing her, checking her knowledge. Every senior doctor did it with subordinates and this was a teaching hospital. Well, she would show him what she was made of.

'Of course. Okay, Tilly, what you're having done today is a radial forearm flap for your tongue cancer. That means we take some tissue from your forearm and use it as a replacement for the tissue we will be removing from your tongue. We use the forearm as it has the terrific advantage of not shrinking when it heals, so that your speech and swallowing will be greatly aided after surgery.'

'Right.'

'We'll use this area here.' Lauren leaned in to indicate the area of forearm near the wrist. 'It tends to be very smooth, doesn't have hair growth and the hole created here on your arm will be covered by a skin graft from either your upper arm or your tummy.'

'Will I be able to use my arm afterwards?'

'It'll be bandaged and held in a special sling for a few days. There will be stitches that will have to come out eventually, and you may feel some tingles or numbness for a few weeks or months because the nerve near the operative site can become bruised, but this should recede with time. Occasionally, it can be permanent, which is a risk, but very rarely does it create pain. Your hand may feel a little weaker to begin with, but we can give you some strengthening exercises and physio and you might notice it feels colder in the winter.'

'That's a lot to take in.'

'It is. If you need more time to decide, we can always postpone your surgery until you feel ready.'

'No. No, I want this done. I want the cancer out.'

Lauren nodded and smiled. 'I understand.'

'Are there any other risks?'

'With surgery there's always the risk of clots, but these are minimal. Maybe two or three per-cent.'

'And what happens then?'

'Well, if it's a drainage clot, the flap can become filled with old blood and you would have to return to Theatre to have the clot removed.'

'But I'd still have the flap?'

'We'd try to preserve it, but if the flap failed we would have to look for other methods of re-construction.'

Tilly looked worried. 'It all sounds rather worrying. I wish I'd not asked now. Ignorance is bliss and all of that. I wish my family were here.'

Lauren understood. It was a scary thing to consider.

'We have to tell you the risks, Tilly, but we'd be remiss to not also tell you the *success rate* for tongue flap surgery. You have no lymph node involvement here. It hasn't spread at all and all your scans are clear. The five-year survival rate for localised tongue cancer is in the mid-eighties and it's much less if you don't have it removed. This is your best option for survival and to give you the ability to talk as well as you can afterwards. We know you're scared. But we're here to help you. Let us look after you. You're in good hands and the other Dr Shaw here is the best in the country.'

Tilly looked at Lauren's ex-husband and smiled. 'I know. I looked him up.' She laughed, a little embarrassed.

'I'd look up my surgeon too,' she whispered conspiratorially.

'Okay!' Tilly sucked in a deep breath. 'Let's do this. When am I up?'

'You're at nine o'clock this morning.'

'Okay.'

'We'll send the anaesthetist in to have a quick chat with you, but next time we see you it'll be in Theatre and then Recovery. Okay?'

Tilly nodded.

Lauren gave her hand a quick squeeze. 'See you in Theatre.'

As they walked away from the patient he realised that Lauren was looking at him in expectation. As if she wanted some sort of feedback from him. He stopped to face her.

'Not bad.'

'Not bad?'

'I think you could have been clearer on one or two things, and I wasn't too happy with you suggesting that she could postpone the surgery. I have a full list for a reason.'

She nodded. 'I'm sure you do; you have great renown. But if a patient isn't ready for surgery, mentally, physically or emotionally, then that can have a drastic effect on healing and recovery times. Especially when we're talking about things like implants or donations. If a patient isn't ready to accept the new change, then—'

He held up his hand. 'I understand the science. I wrote a paper on it.'

She nodded, bristling slightly, feeling that this might be the first of many times the pair of them would lock horns. 'I read it. And it was brilliant and that's why I suggested she take a little more time to think about the surgery if she wasn't ready. It's going to be a huge change for her and I don't think she should be rushed into surgery.'

'Tilly Garson is *ready* for surgery. She's been ready for this surgery ever since she discovered her tongue cancer. Do you know she blamed herself for ignoring the spot on her tongue for three months, because she thought it was an ulcer? That she thought the reason she felt so tired and rundown was because she was stressed, because of her work, and took a sabbatical, even changed her job. That she lost money, not only from work but going on a foreign yoga retreat and on all the home remedies she thought she'd use to try and heal her ulcer, rather than get it checked by a dentist or doctor? She's already fought depression because of that, knowing that because she waited the cancer spread and so she is going to lose a significantly larger portion of her tongue than she would originally have needed if she'd sought help straight away. I know my patient, Lauren, and I know that she is ready. And I resent the implication that I might rush a patient into surgery because it fits *my* schedule, rather than theirs.'

He'd not meant to rail at her, but he couldn't help it. She'd been here minutes and already she was questioning his methods. He knew she wanted to make an impact here, to show what she could do, and he also wanted to see what she could do! But never on this, not on patient care, which he considered himself very conscious of.

Lauren looked subdued. 'I didn't mean to imply anything like that.'

Now he felt bad. The last thing he'd wanted to do was argue with her within half an hour of their meeting. He'd not wanted to argue with her at all! Oliver had wanted nothing more than to show that they were both grown-ups here, having spent a decade apart, and that they were civilised and friendly and adult. And, deep down, he knew she was just trying to show him that she was a well-rounded surgeon, not just someone who wanted to cut all the time but a doctor who considered her patient holistically, who wasn't just there to treat the symptoms, or the cause, but to look at their patient as a whole being and do what was right for them. Her heart was in the right place and there was nothing wrong with Lauren's heart.

'And I didn't mean to give a speech.'

'May I still join you in Theatre?'

'Of course. In fact, I thought I could excise the cancer and you could construct the flap. Show me what you can do. What do you think?'

He was offering her a major part of his surgery, showing her that he trusted her. It was a big gesture, but he also had to see her skills. The last time they'd been in a surgery together she'd only been qualified as a surgeon for a year. He wanted to see how much she'd advanced for himself, even though he'd heard great things about her time at the Great Northern Hospital in Scotland.

He'd just been twitchy because…well…he still couldn't believe the reaction he was having to her presence. He'd thought his feelings for Lauren were consigned to the Finished box. That he'd moved on, built himself a new life. To have her walk in here looking so stunning just reminded him of how he'd felt when they'd first met.

'I'd like that. Thank you.'

He nodded. 'We've time for me to give you a quick tour of theatres and introduce you to the team. And after Tilly we've got a cleft lip and palate surgery to perform on the most perfect four-month-old you have ever seen.'

Her face lit up then. 'I love doing those surgeries. They make such a difference.'

'All of our work makes a difference.'

Lauren smiled. 'I know.' She paused for a moment, looked directly up at him. 'Thank you, Oliver.'

'For what?' He was confused.

She shrugged. 'Just...thank you.'

He didn't know what he was being thanked for. But he did like the way she was looking at him like that. It gave him a warm feeling in his stomach, made his heart thud a little. Made him feel self-deprecating.

'You're welcome, Lauren.'

It felt good to be saying her name out loud again, something he'd not realised he'd missed. Their earlier altercation had passed, it was forgotten. It had simply occurred from the stress of the situation. Of being back together, working together after such a long time apart, establishing positions and roles. Jostling to take their allocated space here. She was beneath him in his department when before, in marriage, they'd been equal. It was always going to be a weird moment. And at least they'd been arguing about patient care, and not about each other.

Hopefully, now, everything else they did with each other would run smoothly.

Lauren had lost count of how many times she'd stood in a scrub room and prepped for a surgery. How many times she had stood at a sink and lathered up with an antimicrobial soap from her fingertips to her elbows, all the while running through the next surgery in her mind as she got her head into the surgical headspace she would need to operate. It was a magical moment. Almost meditative.

But today it felt different, standing next to Oliver as they went through the same procedures to operate together, their first time in Theatre together in over a decade. The last time she'd operated with him, it had been to reposition an upper jaw on a twenty-three-year-old girl and Lauren had only been qualified as a surgeon for a short time. Back then, she'd still been incredibly nervous, grateful for her husband's superior knowledge and skill, knowing he would take the lead and do the majority of the cutting whilst she retracted. But now she would stand by his side as almost his equal. He was still the senior surgeon, but she knew so much more now. She had more experience and was no longer a dewy-eyed novice.

Oliver was going to let her incise and create the forearm flap that would be used to replace the large section of Tilly's tongue being removed for her oral cancer. It was precision work, as a lot of reconstructive surgery was, and she felt thrilled she would be able to show off her skills today.

But she hadn't considered one important thing.

Coming into work this morning for the first time at the Great Southern, she'd assumed that there might be a little awkwardness between her and Oliver. They were divorced, hadn't seen or spoken to each other in ten years—there was bound to be a little tension.

But she'd not expected the sexual tension she'd felt on seeing him that first time. It was as if her body was betraying her...remembering their sex life, how wonderful it had been. Letting her know that he was close by again. She could actually feel a surge in her hormones as her body reawakened being near him. After all this time it was irritating, disruptive to the calm exterior she wanted to present to him.

And it was unexpected. How had he got even more delicious-looking now that he was in his fifties? His scrubs revealed even more than the suit had this morning when she'd met him in Reception. Back there, he'd worn a fitted, long-sleeved shirt. The scrubs revealed the musculature that now lay beneath—sculpted musculature owed to the hours he clearly spent working out now, something that before, when they'd been married, had been an occasional thing, something he'd fitted in around the many hours he'd spent at work.

Lauren had once resented the hours he'd spent at the gym. He was away so long at the hospital as he built his career while she was at home, a young mother to their two daughters. At the end of each day, she'd been desperate for him to come home to her so she could have some adult conversation, or at least feel like the woman she used to be before motherhood changed her, but he would go to the gym, or occasionally meet up with his friends, and she'd resented that. Especially when he'd told her that he'd gone to the gym because he just needed a little time to himself on occasion.

Well, what about her? When had she ever got time to herself, with two small children crawling all over her every day?

She'd tried to not be resentful, but it was hard. He was working for them, he kept saying. Doing all the hours that he could to earn money, because she wasn't able to work back then. She could have gone part-time, but by the time she'd paid for childcare she'd have been working and exhausting herself for nothing and then her children would have suffered. So she'd stayed home, given all of herself to Kayley and Willow, and hoped that on occasion Oliver would have time for her. She'd missed him whilst they'd been married, had stayed quiet much too long, whilst all the time he'd moved further and further away from them, until they'd become like strangers to each other.

But there was no point in admiring him now. He wasn't single. He was with Daria, his much younger girlfriend, and he must look at her now and see all the lines, all the wrinkles, the grey hair. Lauren couldn't compete—nor did she want to—with a thirty-year-old.

'I remember the last time we did this. Scrubbed in together,' she said.

'Me too.'

'You do?'

He nodded. 'Of course. Jane Cavanaugh. Upper jaw surgery.'

She was surprised yet pleased he remembered the patient and the case.

'I saw her again recently. She'd come into the hospital to visit a relative and we met in the corridor. Asked me if I could recommend a plastic surgeon.'

'Plastic surgeon? What for?'

'She'd begun to very much believe that her re-aligned jaw was making her nose more prominent and she wanted it reduced and also to have her upper lip plumped up.'

'Why? She's a beautiful girl!'

'She is. But, from what I could discover, our jaw surgery seemed to set off a trail of later surgeries. She'd also had her breasts done and even went to Turkey for butt implants.'

'Wow. That's a lot of surgeries in ten years.'

'Some people get addicted. They see one fault, they get it fixed and then they just hyperfocus on another part of themselves that they think is wrong.'

'Did she ever get any counselling?'

'I'm not sure. I hope so.'

When they'd finished scrubbing they made their way into Theatre, where nurses helped them into gowns and they put on gloves and went over the list of procedures to ensure they had the correct patient on the table for the correct procedure. Tilly's scans were on a screen and Oliver double-checked these, before going to stand on his side of the table and checking that everything was good on the anaesthetist's end.

He got a thumbs-up from the gas man.

'Okay, we'll make a start.' Oliver proceeded to outline to the theatre staff the procedure they hoped to follow today—that he would operate separately on Tilly's tongue as Lauren worked on the arm to create the flap and collect the skin graft—and once everyone knew who was doing what they began to work.

'Scalpel.'

Tilly's arm was already marked out by Oliver, but Lauren double-checked the markings for herself before she began to cut. The flap needed to be precise and exact if this was to replace a portion of tongue. The flap itself needed to act like the tongue, so that afterwards Tilly would be able to speak as clearly as she could, and so she could eat, so she could swallow. This flap would define her happiness after the surgery. But also, if she did this flap well, then it would show Oliver just how far she had come and where she was destined to go.

Her career had begun many years after his. Her dreams had been put on hold whilst she raised their daughters, and it was her time now. She had lofty goals and wanted to reach the post of consultant, which was possibly within reach in the next couple of years if everything went to plan. And, to do that, she had to show everybody, and not just Oliver, just what kind of surgeon and doctor she was.

She wanted to be exemplary. Extraordinary. She wanted people from around the country, if not from around the globe, to come and seek her out because she was the best—just like they did with Oliver.

'How's it going, Lauren?'

'It's going well. Just working on the blood vessels. What about you?'

'I think I've got clear margins, but Pathology will let me know for sure.' She looked up in time to see him hand a slice of tissue to a nurse. 'Get that to Path, please.' And then he turned back with gauze to dab away any excess bleeding from within the oral cavity before he looked at her. 'Flap looks good. That's excellent.'

'Thank you.' She could see he was smiling at her from behind his mask, crow's feet in the corners of his eyes that had never been there before but now just made him look even more devilishly charming than he ever had.

She felt something stir inside and told herself to concentrate.

It was disconcerting to feel the things for Oliver that she was currently experiencing. Distracting. She'd thought that any feelings she'd ever had for him were dormant after ten years apart, but maybe she ought to have known better. Her relationship with him was over. She'd never expected to awaken anything at seeing him again, yet clearly, her body remembered. And *wanted*. Decades of loving someone could not be so easily erased.

Their sex life had never been a problem. In fact, whenever they'd had a moment—or the energy—to reconnect with one another and they were both actually at home, the sex had always been mind-blowing, frustrations and loneliness being blasted away in moments that felt like ecstasy and reconnecting.

But that reconnection had always been a mirage, a sticking plaster at that point in time to cover the huge cracks that were separating them like an earthquake in a disaster movie. Occasionally they would cling together, choosing to believe that everything was still fine, whilst the world around them crumbled and before too long they were too far apart, unable to reach each other. Eventually, they'd just drifted apart and gone their separate ways.

But, despite all of that, she could still remember, as she stood opposite him now, the way his fingers would feel upon her skin. The trail of his tongue across delicate parts of her. The way they'd enjoyed hours of foreplay, teasing and kissing and tickling and sucking until they finally came together in an explosion of ecstasy that left them both breathless.

I must stop thinking about Oliver's tongue and concentrate on creating a new one for Tilly!

As she transferred the free flap over to Oliver, she watched with a steely focus as he began to attach it to the blood vessels within the mouth. It was delicate, exquisite work and watching Oliver operate was like watching a ballet dancer. He was precision orientated, every move considered, delicate and effortless. But she knew the hours, weeks, months, years of practice that had gone into such work that he could move so purposefully and so expertly and make it look easy. It was a complete and utter turn-on. She was so impressed by his skill and ability.

She needed to focus on her *own* work. So she stopped watching her ex-husband. Stopped thinking about his hands. His fingers.

'Prepping the skin graft.'

'I'd rather you used a skin graft from her stomach. She has good quality tissue there,' Oliver said from behind his mask.

'Of course. No problem.' And he was right. Tilly had good skin there. No stretch marks, no scarring, no blemishing. It was perfect for grafting and didn't take too long to use the dermatome to collect the sample. Lauren concentrated hard as she applied the graft to the site on the arm from where she'd created the free flap and began to attach it into place as a nurse dressed the skin graft site.

When they'd finished, they both stepped away from the table feeling satisfied and happy with the surgery.

'Good job, team. Let's get Tilly to Recovery.'

Lauren followed him back out to the scrub room, where they removed their gloves, gown and mask and dropped them into a bin, before they went back to the sinks to scrub out.

'You did well in there.'

It felt good to hear him validate her. To acknowledge her hard work and her ability. It would have felt good to hear that from any new employer, but to hear it from Oliver in particular felt particularly satisfying.

'Thank you. So did you.'

He laughed good-naturedly. 'Cup of tea before the next one?'

It would have been so easy to say yes. To sit down and chat with him over a drink, catch up. See what was happening in both their lives. But the cleft lip and palate surgery was next and she hadn't had a chance to sit with the patient and examine them yet and she wanted to do that. Wanted to meet the parents too.

'I'd like to check in with the next patient, if you don't mind. I haven't met them yet and if I'm to assist with you I'd like to do my own assessment and introduce myself to the parents.'

He smiled, nodded, flicked the last of the water from his hands and arms before grabbing the paper towels to dry with. 'Of course. Surgery is scheduled in forty minutes. Theatre one.' He gave her one last nod of acknowledgement before leaving the scrub room.

It was as if all the air in the room left with him and she let out a huge breath she hadn't realised she'd been holding.

Working with her ex-husband was always going to be a strain to begin with, but she could see he would make sure that her skills were spot-on and that he would expect nothing but the best from her.

Well, she would show him that he would have no reason to doubt her ability, and she also hoped to show him that she was so good at her job that he would wonder how he had managed all these years without her there, standing by his side. She had been a good mother. A good wife. But she wanted to be an excellent surgeon.

CHAPTER THREE

OLIVER STOOD AT the window, looking out over the hospital gardens below, trying to remember what they'd looked like when they were in full bloom over the summer. Trying to imagine if Lauren had ever looked out at identical gardens at the Great Northern when she'd lived in Edinburgh. The two linked modern hospitals had designed their gardens to be identical and he'd often wondered if those designs were not just identical in shape and size but also in flower choice and placement. Had Lauren watched the wisteria clamber over the trellises? Had she noticed the bloom of the roses? Had she sat at the Peace bench and marvelled at the wonder of the laburnum as it burst into vibrant yellow?

Now, in mid-November, the garden looked a little less alive. Looked after by a team of hospital volunteers, most of it had died back for winter, withering and darkening, losing foliage and stripping itself bare as it entered the festive season.

He'd once loved the run-up to Christmas, loving nothing more than going Christmas shopping with Lauren, hunting for the perfect gift for both of their families and friends. That first Christmas, when they'd first got together, before the girls had arrived, had been the best. He remembered walking through Leicester Square with her, hand in hand, as a church choir belted out Christmas tunes beneath fairy lights. He remembered draping an arm around Lauren's shoulder and pulling her in close and kissing her. They'd been so close, it had been so easy to be with one another. And now so much had changed. So much time had passed. The last few Christmases since the girls had moved out and he'd been living alone had felt strange. Empty.

'Olly? You okay?'

Pulled from his reverie, he turned to see who'd spoken. It was Dylan. Dylan Harper, neurosurgeon. They'd worked together on a few cases recently and become friends.

'Hey. Yeah, I'm good. How about you?'

'Great. You seemed miles away.'

'Just thinking.'

'Wife back?'

Oliver smiled. 'Ex-wife.'

Dylan nodded. 'That's right. How's that going?'

'We've just scrubbed in together.'

'Oh, yikes. And how did that go?'

'Not bad, actually. Just feels strange. We used to be so close once and now there's this huge chasm between us. We worked well together. She's got great skills, but...'

'But it was strange?'

Oliver nodded. 'Yeah. And she looked...' He drifted off, not sure he ought to tell the hospital's playboy how good his ex-wife looked. Dylan's reputation preceded him.

'Stunning?'

He smiled. 'Little bit.'

Dylan laughed. 'Maybe she thought the same thing about you. Maybe she's standing at a window somewhere in this hospital thinking about you.'

'I doubt it. She's off with my next patient. We're about to go in and complete a cleft lip surgery.'

'Awesome.' Dylan checked his watch. 'Look, I gotta go, but you must introduce me to the missus some time.'

'Will do. Take care.'

'You too.' Then Dylan was gone, striding away, carefree and confident.

Oliver wished he could be as carefree as Dylan, but he never had been. He'd always felt the weight of responsibility, ever since he'd entered medical school. He and Lauren had met there, they'd had lots of fun in a relatively short time and then she'd found out she was pregnant and they'd got married quickly and suddenly he was a real adult, expected to do real adult things and grow up quickly, from the fun-loving medical student to becoming a husband. *Father.* Not many other junior doctors had a child toddling around when they started their first hospital post. Not many other juniors had a *second* baby on the way within months of starting their job.

Life had moved way too fast. His marriage had moved way too fast and it had been all he could do to try and keep up. To work for his family, to bring in enough income to support them all. He'd done it all for them. The long hours. The time away. The studying. The hard work. The overtime. Extra shifts. And somehow, along the way, he and Lauren had lost one another, become ships that passed in the night, and when they had had time together he'd felt Lauren's frustrations at not being able to pursue the career that she had wanted, and when their girls had moved out she'd left too.

Only now she was back. Qualified. A reconstructive surgeon, hungry to climb the ladder of success, just the way he had. She had sacrificed her career aspirations to ensure she was a good mother. She had held the fort at home for him, to give him a soft place to land when he'd needed. The least he could do was to teach Lauren all that he knew now, so that he could help her climb.

It was only fair.

Glancing at his wristwatch, he saw that it was time to prep for baby Elliot's surgery.

He gave one last look at the garden and couldn't help but think of how it resembled his marriage. It had withered. Died. But there was still potential for life there. Nurtured correctly, it would bloom with the right input.

And he was determined to help Lauren bloom.

Because it was her time to be in the sun now.

The nurses were starting to decorate for Christmas on the children's ward. An artificial tree was being pulled from its box as Lauren went up to them.

'Excuse me, I'm looking for Elliot Kane.'

A nurse with a lanyard decorated in teddy bears pointed to the left. 'Through there, bed six.'

'Thank you. Is Willow around? Dr Shaw?'

'She's in clinic this morning.'

'Oh, okay.'

It would have been nice to have seen Willow at work. Their younger daughter had followed in her parents' footsteps and become a doctor, a paediatrician. Lauren had come down for her graduation ceremony and celebrated with her, but she'd never actually got to see her daughter at work and see what kind of doctor she was. She expected she was an amazing one. It took a special kind of courage to work with sick kids, day in and day out. Sick children could break your heart and get inside your head way more easily than adult patients did. But Willow had always been a strong young woman. Determined. Hard-headed. Kick-ass. As a young girl, she would often find Willow in her bedroom with a makeshift hospital ward—all her toys, dolls and plushies lying in rows that were meant to be beds, with various bits of toilet paper or tissue wrapped around limbs or heads and Willow pretending to be the doctor taking care of them. It had been quite cute and she'd loved listening to her dad's stories of life in the hospital. So it had been no surprise that she'd gone to medical school like them.

Kayley had been different, however. Their eldest had been fascinated with the law and police shows and murder mysteries and she'd studied law and become a lawyer, specialising in criminal law.

The two girls could not be more different, yet when they were together they got on so well, probably because there was only fourteen months between them.

Lauren headed into the ward, located bed six and headed on over.

There was a young couple sitting next to Elliot's bed, trying to get him to play with a carousel that was turning musically above his bed.

'Mr and Mrs Kane, I'm Dr Shaw. I'll be assisting in Elliot's surgery today. How is he doing?' She looked down at the most beautiful baby she had ever seen. Cleft lip babies were beyond special, with the most amazing smiles.

'He's doing great. He has no idea what's about to happen, does he?' Elliot's mum looked to be on the verge of tears and her husband draped his arm around her shoulder.

'He'll be just fine,' he whispered, hugging her close and stroking his wife's arm.

Lauren watched them together, admiring them. She and Oliver had never had to go through this. Had never seen either of their daughters in a hospital, injured or awaiting surgery. They'd been lucky. Just cuts and scrapes, chicken pox, colds. Nothing like this. Nothing where they had to give up their child to strangers, knowing that they were going to be anaesthetised and cut and stitched and repaired. She couldn't imagine how awful it must be.

'We'll take good care of him. The best. Is it all right if I examine him?'

Elliot's mum nodded.

'Hey, Elliot. My name is Lauren and I'm just going to take a look at your handsome face, okay?' she said in a sing-song voice. Elliot might only be a baby and would not understand anything that she was saying, but Lauren had been trained to explain to every patient, no matter how old or how young, who they were and what they needed to do. It was a respect thing. Just because Elliot was a baby, it didn't matter that he couldn't consent on his own. She would still explain what she was doing.

Elliot burbled back at her, a bubble forming on his lips as he tried to blow a raspberry. It was beyond cute and she kept smiling and making soothing noises as she examined his cleft lip. It was a bilateral complete cleft, meaning that there were openings on both sides that extended up into the nostrils. Technically, it was a relatively easy repair and Lauren knew the parents and Elliot would feel the difference as soon as he came out of Recovery. This was one of those great surgeries that was instant, where a surgeon knew for sure that what they were doing would hugely improve a patient's life.

When her examination was complete she gave Elliot a little hug and handed him over to his mum, who took him gratefully and squeezed him tight, knowing that he would be going to surgery soon.

'Do you have any questions before we take him down to Theatre?'

They shook their heads. 'Just look after him, please, like he's your own,' said the mum.

'Of course.' Lauren reached up to stroke Elliot's soft, downy head, before smiling and heading back to the team. It had felt good to take this break away from Oliver. To just breathe and know that the initial discomfort of seeing him again was now over.

It could only get easier from now on, right?

Even though he'd operated with Lauren this morning already, to see her again in the cleft lip surgery simply reminded him that from now on Lauren was going to be around, here in the hospital, working on some of his cases, working on some of her own. He would see her around and about in the halls, the staffroom, the canteen. They might casually bump into one another in the car park. Share a lift. Share frustrations. Losses. Wins. She was back and she was here and she wasn't his any more.

She wouldn't be at home.

That was the weirdest thing, even though they'd been divorced now for ten years, to have her suddenly back in his life, but knowing that this time she would not be waiting for him at home. It felt strange. Tonight, she would go home to another man. Mike. Who undoubtedly treated her right. She would snuggle on the couch with him. He would put his arm around her. Touch her. Be overfamiliar with her. Sleep with her.

And he'd learned to be okay with that.

He'd learned through Willow and Kayley that their mum was dating another guy, another surgeon, and even though they'd been apart and he was dating too, he'd looked the guy up on the internet. He'd found a picture of Lauren and Mike attending a charity gala and the guy looked like a rock star. Worse still was his impressive resumé, which he'd discovered with a deeper internet search.

He'd told himself to be happy for her. To let her live her life. They were separated now. Divorced. He was no longer allowed an opinion, but he'd still been hurt to imagine that she had replaced him so quickly when he'd believed when they'd first met that they were each other's soulmate. And so he'd thrown himself deeper into work. Then he'd met Daria, and even though she was much younger than him and looking to surge forward in her own career, he'd told himself that what was good for Lauren should also be good for him.

'Tell me the primary function of cleft lip surgery?' he asked her as he began to prepare for the lip repair.

'Function. And aesthetics.'

Her eyes crinkled behind her mask, telling him that she was smiling. He'd always loved her smile. It was warm, welcoming. It made him smile too. Always.

'Function of what?'

'The circular muscles around the mouth, to assist with speech, eating and swallowing.'

'And what are those circular muscles called?' He didn't mean to drill her as he incised the cleft. But this was a teaching hospital and she was here to develop as a reconstructive surgeon and if she was going to be working on his team then he needed to know her knowledge base was strong on the basics, at least. A lot of doctors thought they could skip the basics, but they were there for a reason.

'The orbicularis oris muscle.'

'Good. And what happens after I close the orbicularis oris muscle?'

'It creates a philtral ridge to complete the philtrum.'

She knew her stuff and he gave her an appraising look over the table. She wasn't looking at him but at the operating site, those blue eyes of hers...so warm, so bright. *Beautiful.*

Suddenly aware that he must have paused, Lauren looked up at him.

He looked back down at baby Elliot and asked

the theatre nurse for the sutures. 'And what kind of sutures would we use in the repair of a cleft lip?'

'Er…it depends on the area being stitched. A simple interrupted suture on the vermilion edge or a vertical mattress suture on the philtrum.'

'And on the cupid's bow?'

'Tip stitch suture.'

He nodded. She did know her stuff. 'Good.' He passed her the sutures. 'Get to it.'

She smiled at him, the way she had in the good old days, as if they were sharing a private joke, and she took the sutures from him and began to work.

'More light, please,' she asked the theatre nurse to adjust the large light above them so that she could see better as she now worked.

He watched her carefully, her concentration. The way a small crease formed between her brows. The way her small, delicate hands worked niftily and neatly. She was quick. Purposeful. Knowledgeable. But, most importantly, she was skilled. She wasn't nervous working in front of him. Her hands didn't tremble or shake because he was watching and he couldn't help but admire her for that. He'd had many students work with him in surgeries, or newly registered surgeons, who trembled to work in his presence. But not Lauren.

There'd always been a strength in her. A core of steel. There'd had to be, raising their two daughters alone, putting her career on the backburner so that he could work all the hours he could to provide for them, whilst she'd dealt with everything else. She'd been his rock and his security and he'd simply trusted that she would always be there.

Until she wasn't. And he'd realised, quickly, that he'd taken her for granted. Stopped seeing her. Only realising just what he had lost when she'd packed her bags and moved out.

'I think I'm done.'

He looked down at the neat stitches. She'd done a marvellous repair, just how he would have done it.

'Great job.'

'Thank you.'

'You're welcome.' He smiled back at her, wondering what kind of surgeon she'd be right now if he'd been the one to stay at home and look after the kids and she'd been the one to work on her career. No doubt she'd be head of her own department by now.

'Let's get Elliot to Recovery, please, Nurse.' He pulled off his gloves and mask and gown, dumping them in the clothing bin before heading into the scrub room to wash down.

Lauren followed him in. 'Thank you for letting me close up. I appreciate that.'

'No problem.'

'I'm glad that we can be adult about all of this and work well together. It's not going to be a problem, is it?'

A problem? No. It was more than that. It was disturbing to have her here again. To be so close. To be so wonderful. Gorgeous. Sexy. A painful reminder of what he'd once had. What he'd lost. It reminded him of his foolishness. Of his mistakes. His pride. His whole body and mind reacted to her being in the room. To being beside him. Opposite him. Close to him. Smelling as wonderful as she did, looking as beautiful as she was. Her skill clear to see, her natural ability now allowed the free rein it had deserved all those years ago. He felt guilty for stopping her from being who she could be.

'Of course not. No problem at all.' He hoped he sounded convincing.

CHAPTER FOUR

THE HOSPITAL CANTEEN was busy, humming with voices and busy people going this way and that. Lauren picked up a tray and chose an egg mayo salad sandwich and a small slice of strawberry cheesecake for her dessert, along with a pot of tea, and then began the tedious task of trying to find a free table.

The canteen was open to both the staff and the public so there was a mix of people and she scanned the faces to see if she could see who she had arranged to meet.

Willow, her daughter. Dr Willow Shaw, a newly qualified paediatrician.

Their youngest daughter had her father's features. Long, dark hair that was silky-smooth and glossy. Green eyes, the same as her father. The only thing she seemed to have inherited from her mother was her small stature and the slight upturn that she had to her nose. Beyond that, she was all Oliver.

Her gaze scanned the crowd and eventually

she noticed a raised hand at the back and the smiling face of her daughter.

Lauren beamed and made her way over, edging between diners and visitors until she made it to the table. She set down her tray and her daughter stood and they gave each other a big hug.

It had been four months since they'd last seen each other in person. Whilst up in Edinburgh, Lauren had tried to video call her daughters at least once a week, which was nice and had made Lauren feel that she wasn't missing out on too much, but it wasn't the same as actually being here. Actually being able to hold them and squeeze them and love them in person.

'Oh, this is nice,' Lauren said, still hugging her daughter tight. Willow smelt lovely, wearing a lightly scented perfume that seemed floral and her hair smelling of coconut. 'I've missed this.'

'Me too.'

They eventually let go, despite Lauren wanting to hold Willow close to her for ever, and sat down opposite one another. It had felt good to hug someone. Since seeing Oliver that morning and feeling such a visceral reaction, her body had needed contact and as she couldn't hug him, hugging her daughter whom she hadn't seen for four months was just as good.

Willow had an iced coffee and looked to be

halfway through a jacket potato covered in chilli and cheese.

'That looks good,' she said, feeling a little less optimistic about her sandwich and wishing now that she'd gone for a hot meal.

'It's not bad. You know hospital food.'

'I do.' Lauren wrinkled her nose and laughed. 'So how are you? Settling in to your new job?'

'I'm doing great! Really enjoying it, and my team are fantastic. Lots of friendly faces, which is what you need in Paeds. How about you?' Willow leaned in, almost conspiratorially. 'How did it go with Dad? Have you met up yet?'

Lauren felt a flush of heat suffuse her body at the thought of Oliver, at how well it had gone today. At least to outward appearances. Anybody watching them would never have known of the turmoil she was feeling inside at how she had physically reacted to seeing Oliver again today. Of how all the memories had come flashing back.

'We have, yes. We've even operated together.'

'Ooh! Tell me everything.'

'There's not much to tell. We operated on a tongue cancer patient and created a new flap from her arm and then we worked on a cleft lip baby.'

'Two surgeries?'

Lauren nodded and took a bite of sandwich,

not because she was hungry but because it stopped her from saying all the things she was feeling.

Your father looked amazing and I found myself checking him out. You never told me he's turned into a silver fox. I found myself reacting to him, physically. Like I wanted him—actually wanted him! Some remnant of lust or something that my body felt, which clearly hasn't got the message that we're divorced.

'Well, you must have talked about something.'

Lauren nodded, still chewing. 'This and that. Mainly about the patients, but we did seem to get on and we've both agreed that it isn't going to be a problem, us working together.'

'Oh.'

Lauren smiled. 'You sound strangely disappointed. Aren't you happy that your father and I are getting along?'

'Of course I am! I just… I don't know. You haven't seen each other in ten years and have always managed to avoid each other at birthday parties and celebrations—all carefully co-ordinated, no doubt. I just thought there might have been more when you met up with each other again. Do you think he's changed?'

Of course she did. Oliver was more honed. Physically stronger. Sexier. The young puppy fat days had passed and made him leaner and chiselled and deliciously edible-looking!

'A little.'

'Does he know about Mike yet?'

'I haven't told him. Have you?'

'I figured it was your news to share.'

'I'll tell him when the time is right.'

She didn't want Oliver to find out about it and read too much into it. Lauren had made the choice to move back down south to be with her family again. She'd missed Kayley and Willow so, so much. Video calls just weren't cutting it any more and they were all getting so busy, Willow working long hours as a junior doctor and Kayley putting all the hours into her job as a criminal lawyer. There'd been too many times when they'd missed their calls with one another or postponed them, and Lauren had begun to feel as if she was being edged out of their lives and she'd hated that feeling.

She'd wanted to be there with them, close to them if they needed her, and the job at the Great Southern had just happened to open up. It had made perfect sense to her to leap at it, despite the fact that she'd known she would be working with her ex. But their divorce had been quite amicable in the end. They'd both been adult about it, there was no reason why they couldn't work in the same hospital. After all, it was a big place with plenty of room for both of them. And she'd honestly believed that meeting up with Oliver again might be difficult but manageable. It wasn't as if they were dramatic teenagers who'd had a massive falling-out and hated each other. They'd drifted apart over the years, pulled in different directions, and they were proper adults now. In their fifties! Even if sometimes Lauren still felt like she was in her twenties.

She couldn't believe the years had gone by. When she was younger, she remembered celebrating her own mother's fiftieth birthday. She'd wanted a huge celebration and a big fuss made of her and Lauren, aged sixteen at the time, had thought how *old* her mother was!

She didn't feel that way now, realising her own mother had *never* been old at fifty. There'd still been plenty of years left in her. Indeed there still were.

'I guess there's a little part of me that's kind of hopeful about my parents being back in each other's life. That I'll no longer be from a broken home.' Willow grinned and spooned in a mouthful of chilli.

Lauren laughed. 'You're hoping for a grand reunion, are you?' She flushed at the thought, her brain helpfully presenting her with an image of her and Oliver stumbling into an empty linen cupboard as they raked at each other's clothes, kissing madly and having a passionate make-out session in there, like the ones she saw in her favourite hospital drama on television.

'Is that so wrong?' She was still smiling.

'Totally. Your father and I are different people now.'

'Exactly.' Willow pointed at her with her fork. 'You're both in a place, career-wise, where you've always wanted to be. You don't have the stresses and strains of raising a family any more. Kayley and I are grown up, doing grown-up things. I'm engaged to be married and Kayley already is! We're making our own families now. You and Dad have time to do what you want to do.'

'I'm focused on my career, Wills, that's all. It's my first day and I want to make a good impression, not just on your father but on *everyone*.'

'Doesn't mean you can't have a bit of fun. Hashtag just saying.' Willow smiled.

Lauren smiled back. 'I can have fun *without* your father. Hashtag just saying.' It was their little in-joke with one another. 'Anyway, how is Kayley? I haven't heard from her in a while.' Her oldest daughter had been strangely quiet recently.

Willow shrugged. 'She's a bit down.'

'Because of the baby thing?' Kayley and her husband, Aaron, had been trying to get pregnant since they got married a couple of years ago. There'd been one pregnancy early on, discovered a week or two after they got back from their Caribbean honeymoon, but it had resulted in a miscarriage at six weeks that had devastated them both. Since then, they'd been trying to get pregnant again, to no avail.

'Yeah. She calls me each time her period arrives, usually in tears. It's got to the point where I just don't know what to say to her any more. All my platitudes are empty, you know?' Willow pushed her plate away.

'She calls me too. Didn't they go away on that couples retreat thing? I remember her telling me about it, but I've not heard from them since. She's always busy, it seems. I wonder if she could lessen her stress a little it might help?'

'Maybe. Sometimes I feel she gets a little angry with me when we speak.'

'Why?'

'Because I'm a doctor. And so are you and so is Dad and yet doctors haven't been able to tell her why she can't fall pregnant. Sometimes I get the feeling she blames us.'

'I guess she has to direct her anger and frustrations somewhere. And if that's what she needs then I'll let her do it. Has Oliver spoken to her recently?' Oliver had always been Kayley's favourite. When she was little, if she had a fall and scraped her knee, Lauren would patch her up but it would be Oliver's knee she would clamber on when he finally made it home.

'He hasn't said anything. But maybe he hasn't heard from her either. She has been a little AWOL these last few weeks.'

'Maybe I should ask him?'

The thought of breaching the professional barrier she had with her ex-husband right now was terrifying, though. Because if she suddenly took their relationship from professional to personal, initiated a closer connection than they'd been pretending, then maybe that would be dangerous, considering the unexpected feelings she'd had for him since they'd met again. Because Lauren could not deny the zing she'd felt at seeing and being with him again.

'You could try.' Willow checked the time. 'Wow. How come lunch breaks go so fast?'

'It's a strange anomaly in hospital time. All breaks, lunch or otherwise, go much faster than shifts. What sort of cases have you got at the moment? Anything interesting?'

'The usual. Nothing exciting or terrifying, which is good. You?'

'I'm sitting in on your dad's clinic this afternoon for an hour or so, just to see how things get processed here and then, excitingly, I get to run the clinic and meet a couple of new patients of my own.'

'Sounds great.' Willow made to stand. 'You must let me know how that goes. And if you hear from Kayley you'll let me know?'

'Of course.' She stood as well to give her daughter another hug. 'We must do this again soon.'

'Absolutely. Now, enjoy your sandwich whilst you can.' Willow kissed her on the cheek, gathered her plate on its tray and headed towards the exit.

Lauren found herself sitting alone and worrying about Kayley. She had been *in absentia* lately and she worried that maybe her daughter was getting so wrapped up in trying for a baby that she was losing herself in the process. It could affect people that way sometimes and she didn't blame them for it. She could recall sitting with Kayley once, a few weeks before her wedding, and the gleam in her eyes when she'd said they would start trying for a baby as soon as the ring was on her finger.

'And it'll probably happen really quickly. I mean, you had no problem, Mum. You just had to sit on the same couch as Dad and you'd get pregnant!'

And they'd both laughed and laughed, because it had seemed true at the time. Lauren had fallen pregnant so quickly, so easily, there was no reason to think that Kayley would have a problem.

And she had fallen pregnant once, after her honeymoon, and Kayley and Aaron had been ecstatic, telling everyone. They'd both been so happy, so proud. And then that phone call, late one evening, from Aaron. Kayley was likely miscarrying, bleeding heavily. A doctor had confirmed it. Kayley had sunk into quite a depression. It had been hard to watch, but slowly, over time, she'd picked up and been ready to try again and the whole family had been hopeful, as Kayley and Aaron were, that it would happen quickly again. And each month had ticked by with disappointment after disappointment, so much so that Kayley had begun to find it difficult to face any of them. She seemed to feel she carried the blame, when that blatantly wasn't true. No one was to blame.

But where was she? *How* was she?

And why had no one heard from her for a while?

Oliver had chosen not to eat in the hospital canteen today for lunch. He'd known that Willow was meeting with her mum there and if he'd arrived at the same time their daughter would have called him over too and expected them to eat lunch together like old times, and he wasn't sure he was ready to do that.

He'd already spent plenty of time with Lauren this morning and he just needed a little breather, a little fresh air, to get his head straight. Reset. Recalibrate. Discover a way he could be with his ex-wife so that he wasn't thinking about her hair, or the way her eyes still shone so bright and so blue that he remembered how dark they would go whenever they were being intimate. Because it was wrong to think of her in that way any more. She wasn't his. They'd divorced. Remembering their more passionate moments whilst standing next to her now was a little off, wasn't it?

And so he'd headed out of the hospital and made it to a local sandwich truck and allowed himself to indulge in a totally unhealthy all-day breakfast sandwich filled with sausage and bacon and egg. He didn't often allow himself a cheat day but he'd not had one for a while, so why not? It had been a stressful day and it still wasn't over. But at least if he could just get through the next few hours, then after that Lauren would be free to do more of her own thing. She had three patients of her own that were coming in later on this afternoon and he'd be able to stop being her teacher for the day.

He was looking forward to that and he had

to believe that Lauren was looking forward to it too. She did not want to be chained to her ex-husband's side, right?

'Olly?'

He turned at the voice. 'Daria, hey.'

His relationship with Daria had ended some time ago, but it still felt strange to run into her again. Was this his day for meeting exes?

'Long time, no see.'

'It is. Are you here at the hospital on business or…?' Daria was a drug rep. She'd turned up at his office once to try and sell him on some new skin cream that was supposedly revolutionary in its ability to assist with reducing scarring after surgery and there'd been a bit of a spark between them. At first he'd thought she was just doing a little flirting to make a deal with him on the skin cream, but then she'd asked him out for a drink. He'd accepted and the rest was history.

'Business.'

'Ah. Who are you here to see?'

'I have an appointment with Dr Dylan Harper.'

Oliver smiled. The hospital playboy. Dylan wasn't really a playboy; he just had the reputation for it. He was a good-looking guy. Probably Daria's type?

'Well, I'll let you get to it then. Take care.'

He began to walk away, but then she called after him, 'I heard your wife is back.'

He turned. '*Ex-wife*. And how did you hear about that?'

Daria smiled. 'I have connections. Connections talk and get gossipy when they've had a few drinks in a wine bar.'

He nodded. 'Nothing faster than the hospital grapevine.'

'What's it like, having her back?'

'It's fine.'

She smiled, tilted her head to one side as if she didn't believe him. 'Come on!'

'What?'

'The woman you loved, who you've had two daughters with, is suddenly back in your life after a decade or so. You must have some feelings about it.'

'Well, if I do, they're certainly nothing to do with you. But it's nice to see you looking so well, Daria. Have a nice day.' He raised his coffee cup as a goodbye and strode away from her, determined not to give her any more of his time or attention.

Daria had been great to begin with, but very quickly he had begun to feel like a portal through which she could shop her products. She'd seemed to want to use him to create further contacts and her flirting with other doctors was so off the scale that he'd begun to hear rumours. So it had been easy to end it before it had become something more, not that he could ever have imagined his relatively short time with Daria as anything that could have become serious. She'd not been after that and neither had he. Short flings had not turned out to be his thing. He was a guy who valued commitment and the long-term.

Upon arrival at his clinic he noticed Lauren waiting for him. She hadn't seen him yet, but she stood leaning against the wall worrying at a nail. The action made him smile. He'd forgotten how she used to do that when she was worrying about something. He'd always thought it cute. With a smile on his face, he walked up to her.

'Missed lunch?'

She started and flushed pink, embarrassed at having been caught. 'Oh! Sorry.' She pushed off away from the wall as he unlocked the door with a swipe of his NHS ID card and let them both in. 'And no, I had lunch. I met with Willow.'

'How's she getting on?'

'Good! Good. We had a nice time, though we spent half of it worrying about Kayley. I haven't heard from her in a long time and neither has she. Have *you* heard from her?'

'Er…she rang me about ten days ago, said she was going away with Aaron for a break. Somewhere abroad—Croatia, I think. I would have said if I'd known that you were all worrying about her.'

'So she's fine, then? If she's gone on holiday.'

'I think it was more of a retreat.'

'But you felt that she was fine?'

He shrugged. In all honesty, he'd felt as if there was something she wasn't saying, something she couldn't tell him, and he'd not wanted to push her on it, knowing she would tell him when she was ready. But did he want to keep that tiny nugget from Lauren? He didn't want to hurt her and he already knew she felt it keenly that Kayley was closer to him than she was to her mother.

'I think she just wanted some time alone with her husband. Away from the stresses of home and all her disappointments.'

'Her disappointments? You mean not getting pregnant? The miscarriage?'

'Maybe. I don't know. I did feel like she had something she wasn't saying, so maybe they've gone for a treatment at some spa or special fertility clinic?'

Lauren was pacing. 'But she's got a good head on her shoulders. She wouldn't have gone for some radical treatment abroad without researching it first, would she?'

He could tell that Lauren was getting super stressed by this idea and he reached out to stop her pacing and laid a hand on her arm to calm her, to stop her, without thinking. It was an old habit.

She looked at him in surprise and he let go, his hand pulling away quickly as if he'd just been burned. Her look had said *You're overstepping the mark*. He'd not meant to. It had just happened. Touching her in such a familiar way…it did strange things to his head.

'She's a sensible girl and we have to trust her.'

Lauren was still looking perturbed by his touching her. So much so, he wondered if he ought to apologise for overstepping a boundary, but then she spoke.

'I just wish she'd spoken to me about it.' To stop herself pacing, she sank into the chair opposite his desk, where the patient would sit.

He did the logical thing and went around his desk so that it lay between them like a large metallic barrier, the perfect wall, creating an expanse from which he could not touch her.

'I know you're worried about her, we all have been. But you've got to allow her to live her life the way she and Aaron decide.'

'I know but… I came all this way to be with my girls and I haven't seen her at all…and now she's gone away? When is she coming back, did she say?'

He shook his head, knowing his answer would disappoint her. He hated seeing her worrying about this. Hated seeing her sad. It simply reminded him of how he'd made her feel in the past and the guilt that had followed and he wanted to make her smile. This was Lauren's time to be happy, not sad.

'I can see you're worrying about all of this but there's not much we can do right now. Instead of you going home and worrying about it, why don't you come out for dinner tonight? We can talk, catch up on family and work and the hospital now that there are three of us that work here.' He smiled, softening the offer, letting her know he wasn't asking her out on a date. It was just family stuff. Adulting stuff. More of a formality, really, than anything else.

She looked at him, surprised, then nodded.

He wasn't sure she'd accept, but when she did he felt inordinately pleased. Good food always made a tense situation better. And if he took her to the right place he might be able to make her smile and forget her worries.

Not that he wasn't worried about Kayley too. It was just that he knew his daughter and he knew that if she had anything to tell them she would.

When she was ready.

CHAPTER FIVE

LAUREN SAT IN clinic with Oliver, trying to focus on the patients that came in through the doors, but she had a lot swirling around her head. That her own clinic would start in a little over an hour and she'd be set free to start establishing herself here. That she was sitting in this room with her ex-husband, who looked delicious, and his rapport with patients was clear to see. The women adored him. The men admired him. He gave them confidence in their surgical choices, he gave brilliant advice on medical matters and they all left with a smile. He was the ultimate professional. He looked good, sounded good. Smelt good.

She thought and worried about Kayley, wondering what was happening with their eldest daughter, and hoped that she was enjoying herself in Croatia with Aaron. Maybe the relaxed time away would do them some good.

She thought about the casual way Oliver had touched her arm when she was pacing and the lightning bolt of awareness that had rocketed through her body. She'd almost gasped. And she thought about the fact that she had accepted an invitation to dinner with him. Dinner! When she'd started this morning she'd not for one minute thought when she entered the hospital doors that she would have accepted an offer from Oliver to join him for dinner that evening. The most she'd hoped for was that they would be civil to one another, for the sake of the patients, their work colleagues and their daughters.

Dinner! It wasn't a date. It never could be—he was with Daria and, besides, they'd been divorced for years, it had been over a long time ago, but there was still a part of her that was thrilled at the idea. Terrified. Nervous. But she calmed herself by telling herself that it was simply a catch-up. It was sensible. Best to get it out of the way. That Daria would be there too, obviously, because she couldn't imagine her being thrilled by her boyfriend going out for dinner with his ex-wife alone, and surely Oliver wouldn't lie to her about where he was going, so it was all going to be above board, right?

She'd watched Oliver advise a patient on a future sinus surgery, a case to realign a lower jaw, advise another patient on the removal of a benign mass that was growing behind their left eye, and then suddenly they were on break and he was turning to her, smiling.

'So do you feel ready to go and do this on your own?'

'Yes, of course.' She felt more than ready. She'd run her own clinics at the Great Northern and she was looking forward to getting her own surgical list here. Oliver had shown her the computer system, how to log notes, but there wasn't anything new to pick up on—the two hospitals used the same system.

'Good. Fancy a coffee before you start?'

She didn't want to get overly familiar with him. They had pretty much spent all day together already and they would be dining out together tonight, so she shook her head. 'I'd like to get set up in my clinic room, if you don't mind?'

'Of course not. You go ahead.' He smiled. 'But we should get together at the end of clinic so you can fill me in on your cases and what's been decided.'

He was her boss, so it seemed reasonable enough.

'Sure thing.'

'You know where to find me.'

'I do.' She gave him one last smile, thanked him and left the room, once again letting out a huge breath of tension that had been building. She headed to her own clinic room next door to his. It was bland, like most clinic rooms, set up with a desk, computer, chair, a set of cupboards containing the medical basics, a weighing scale, a height measure on the wall and an examining couch with a roll of blue paper.

Lauren let out a sigh of satisfaction, feeling as if her proper work was about to begin. So far today, she'd been guided, assessed, observed. Now was her moment to launch from the safety of the nest and fly free. Booting up the computer, she sat down and began to arrange her desk the way she wanted it.

A knock on her door and the lady from Reception came in with a clipboard that listed her patients and their ID numbers, so she could bring up their notes on screen.

'Would you like a hot drink, Dr Shaw?'

'Yes, please, that would be lovely, Shana, thank you.'

Lauren brought up the case notes for her first patient. Callie Mackenzie needed breast reconstruction after a double mastectomy. She'd fought cancer twice now and had been in remission for three years and felt ready to face surgery again after a few difficult procedures. Lauren was looking forward to hopefully making this woman feel better about herself, whether she chose to go through with the procedure or not.

As Shana brought in her tea, her computer

system let her know that Callie had arrived. Lauren took a fortifying sip of her hot drink, took one last look around her room and then pressed the button that would notify Callie in the waiting room that it was her time to come in. She stood and waited to greet her first ever patient at the Great Southern.

When she walked in, Lauren was gratified to see a woman not cowed by her past battles but one who emanated happiness, from the bright, broad smile on her face to her elegant way of dress, fashionable pixie cut and expensive perfume that filled the room. Callie shook her hand and said hello, before settling herself down into a chair, with another woman at her side.

'Pleased to meet you. I'm Dr Shaw.'

'Callie. Evie,' Callie introduced her partner.

'Okay, so you're here because I received a letter from your GP, indicating that you're interested in reconstructive breast surgery.'

'Yes, that's right.'

'And you had a double mastectomy just over four years ago?' Lauren double-checked the record.

'Yes. I could have had reconstruction at the time of the mastectomy, but I chose not to. The doctor told me it would be safe, but I just wasn't ready, you know? I'd lived with the idea that my breasts were trying to kill me and I just wanted them gone.'

'I understand.' Lauren smiled. 'But you feel ready now?'

'I do.' Callie reached for Evie's hand. 'I have a new partner in my life. I'm happy and I want to feel like a woman again, make my clothes look better on me. Have greater confidence.'

'Wonderful.' Lauren led her through the options for reconstruction, discussed sizes, expanders, showed her a variety of implants, from saline to silicone or even autologous, using tissue from elsewhere in the body.

'I was a thirty-four B before. I think I'd like to stay around that size. Maybe go up to a C? I'd hate to go too big. I need to think about what will suit my frame.'

'Absolutely.' Lauren examined Callie, to check her old incisions. There'd be no problem with expanding her tissue.

'What about nipples?'

Lauren smiled. There weren't many jobs where people could ask that question out loud and be taken seriously.

'Well, we usually wait until you've healed from the reconstruction before we start to construct a nipple and areola. We create a nipple from skin used in the reconstruction and then, a few months after that, we can either tattoo on an areola or use a skin graft from the groin at the time of the nipple reconstruction to create an areola then.'

'I think I'd like as few procedures as possible. I don't particularly enjoy staying in hospital.'

'So you'd prefer areola and nipple reconstruction at the same time?'

Callie glanced at Evie and they both nodded in agreement.

'All right, that shouldn't be a problem.'

Lauren discussed with them surgical aftercare, timeframes, risk factors to the surgery and any complications that could arise as a result of the procedure, but Callie and Evie seemed happy with everything.

'I can't thank you enough,' said Callie. 'You go through these huge life-changing events and always come out a little changed on the other side. It'll be nice to come into hospital for something positive, rather than negative. I'm rebuilding myself.' She smiled.

'We all need a little rebuilding, I think,' agreed Lauren.

She'd been through a lot of changes herself in life. Having two small children close together. Dropping out of medical school to be a mother. Pressing pause on her career aspirations, watching her husband climb rapidly through the ranks in a career she'd wanted for herself. Divorce.

House moves, isolation faraway from family. Starting medical school again and feeling ancient as the oldest in her class and never quite fitting in with everyone else. Being cheated on. Starting again. Having to work under her ex-husband. Worrying about her daughters. At least Kayley and Willow were healthy, right? They'd not had to face the traumas that Callie had. Kayley might be facing tough fertility issues, but she wasn't facing cancer or chemo or radiation or surgery to take away her womb or her breasts.

Maybe I need to stop worrying so much about her. She'll be okay. She has us.

Lauren said goodbye to Callie and Evie and typed up her notes to update the record electronically and then used the voice recorder that would be used to create Callie's letter to her GP.

Her first consult here at the Great Southern was over and now she could move onto the next.

She tried *not* to think that with every patient seen it would bring her closer and closer to her dinner with Oliver.

Oliver wasn't sure how to dress for his meal with Lauren. He didn't want to dress too smartly as he wasn't sure he wanted Lauren to think that he thought that this was a date. Because it wasn't. They were just going to catch up, talk about the girls. About work. About careers. They would talk about how they were both going to navigate this situation they now found themselves in, because he'd never thought for one moment that he would end up as her boss. Well, her senior, anyway. He wasn't head of the department yet, but that was surely only a matter of time.

Phillip Thomson, the current head of department, had already started talking about his retirement coming up in six months' time and the gossip was that Oliver was the front-runner for the post. Even Phillip had told him that he would like Oliver to take over. He'd told him in the same conversation when he'd revealed that he'd interviewed new candidates for the reconstructive surgeon post and offered it to Oliver's ex-wife. That had been one hell of an afternoon!

Oliver stood in front of his wardrobe, trying to decide between a black shirt to go with his black trousers, or whether to go with a white one. Preferring the black, he shrugged that on and began to fasten the cuffs.

He wasn't the man that he'd once been and he couldn't help but remember the first time he'd spotted Lauren at medical school from across a crowded lecture hall. If he remembered correctly, it was a lecture on the peripheral nervous system and Lauren had been concentrating hard, writing notes with a pen that had a fluffy pink ostrich feather on the end that had made him smile, wondering how on earth she could concentrate with that on the end of it. It kept catching his eye, although her long blonde hair had curtained her face until that one moment when she'd tucked her hair behind her ear and he'd been stunned by how beautiful she was.

For the rest of the lecture he'd stolen glances at her and when it was over he'd managed to follow her out, bump into her and ask her what she'd thought of the lecture. When she'd turned those beautiful blue eyes of hers upon him he'd felt winded. And when she'd smiled he'd almost been struck dumb. He'd stuttered an answer to her question in return, laughed, blushed and then bluntly asked her out for a drink. And the rest was history.

He checked his reflection in the mirror and tweaked his hair, which was more silver now than the dark brown locks he used to have. But he cut a decent figure, he thought. He looked after himself these days, had begun filling his spare hours away from the hospital with hours at the gym, or running. He'd done three London Marathons now and was planning his fourth, having caught the running bug. He was leaner, more muscular, and could almost see abs if he sucked in his breath and tensed his stomach muscles!

Oliver checked his watch. He'd promised to

meet her outside a pub they both knew, so they could have a drink first and then head on out to find a nice restaurant and grab a bite to eat.

It was time to go and he felt nervous again. As nervous as he had on their first date, when they'd gone to see a movie and then gone dancing afterwards. He'd not been a great dancer, not yet fully confident in his body, and she'd laughed good-naturedly at him, laughter that had lit up her eyes, and she'd pulled him close and they'd shared their first kiss.

He'd liked to tell everyone that he was lost to her at that first kiss, but that was never quite the whole truth. The moment he'd been lost to her had been the moment she'd tucked her hair behind her ear in that lecture, a moment that he often thought of fondly. He'd been a fool to lose her, but he'd thought he was doing the right thing in working so hard to provide for his rapidly growing family. How many other junior doctors had two young daughters and a wife to provide for? Not many, he'd wager. And he'd lost her for a very long time. It was quite surreal to have her back here, working as a surgeon, following the dream she'd always held close to her heart.

'I'll do it one day, Oliver, just you see. When the girls are older and more settled in school, I'll go back.'

'*Good for you*,' he'd once said—rather patronisingly, he now felt.

But the girls had never got settled in school. Kayley had struggled with dyslexia and Willow with ADHD that she'd masked in bad behaviour. Lauren was always getting called in to speak to headteachers or tutors or pastoral workers and though Kayley's issue had been diagnosed relatively early, everyone had thought that Willow was just acting up because all the focus had been on her older sister.

Of course that had never been the case at all. She'd just struggled to fit in to the strict, ordered timetable of school, forced to learn about subjects in which she had no interest, though she'd excelled in science and especially biology and chemistry.

'*I'm going to be a doctor one day, like Dad,*' she'd said.

His gaze went to a picture he had of the two girls on his bedside table, Willow in her graduation gown, Kayley standing next to her, arm around her shoulders, incredibly proud. His girls had fought so hard to get where they were now, and Lauren had fought for them every step of the way.

He caught a taxi to the pub and waited outside. It was cold and he could see his breath freezing in the air as all around him the street glowed in the lamplight. His teeth chattered a little due to his nerves and he kept stamping his feet so he could keep the feeling in his toes and he was just rubbing his palms together when another taxi pulled up and Lauren stepped out.

It was as if he saw her in slow motion, alighting from the vehicle with all the grace of a royal, her red heels connecting with the ground as she stepped out, revealing her beautiful red dress and the ivory-coloured wrap that she wore about her shoulders. She was laughing at something the driver said and he felt a weird stab of jealousy as Lauren gave him a cash tip and waved him goodbye.

There's no Mike.

Then she turned to face him and smiled and it was as if all was well again as she came towards him, practically gliding, her hair smooth and silken, her eyes smoky and dark.

'Hi. You look great,' he said rather lamely, but he couldn't say all the other things that ran through his mind. Some of them were rather X-rated considering the way that dress hugged her shapely womanly curves and he was too busy trying to calm his runaway heart and his traitorous loins. 'Thought we'd grab a drink first, if that's okay?'

'Perfect.'

Another smile and it was all he could do to

step back and hold the pub door open for her, and though the air that whooshed past smelt of hops and beer and cooked food, when *she* walked past him it was all he could do not to let his mouth drop open and have his tongue roll across the floor like a cartoon character.

She smelt *divine.* Floral. Feminine. Dainty, somehow.

His Baby Bird.

Male eyes turned her way when she entered, he noticed as he followed behind and placed his hand on the small of her back as he guided her towards the bar.

The hand said, *She's mine. Back off.*

His brain logically reminded him otherwise.

CHAPTER SIX

'I HAVE TO say I felt quite nervous about coming out here tonight,' Lauren said, gratefully sipping at the white wine before her.

Oliver had chosen a booth for them to sit in, close to the roaring open fire. It was a welcome heat after the cold outside, where the air had begun to freeze and she knew that in the morning there would be a definite frost, a coating of icy white that would sparkle and glisten. The fire warmed her and stopped her legs from trembling. She wore sheer tights with the dress but had wished, after stepping out of her taxi, that she'd worn trousers instead.

But something inside her, getting ready for tonight, had told her to go all out and dress well for this meeting. Out here, away from the hospital, he was no longer her senior. He was just Oliver, her ex-husband, and there was a small, devilish part of her that wanted to dress up and show him what he was missing. Plus, she also knew she couldn't compete with Daria, who was younger, slimmer and who no doubt had less lines on her face and body as she was still just thirty years old. She just wanted to feel good and to that end she'd even put on her best underwear, even though she knew he'd never get to see it. But it made her feel good. Pulling things in, pushing things up, presenting herself in the best light.

Oliver smiled. 'Me too. It's all a bit strange this, really, isn't it?'

Lauren nodded. 'More than strange. Today was how I always imagined our lives would be, both of us working together at a hospital. I just never suspected it would be this way and all these years later. Anyway, how have you been?'

'I'm good. And you?'

'Yes, great. How are things with Daria?' Lauren tried not to sound bitter in any way.

'Fine, I guess. She was here today, actually. To see another doctor, not me.'

Lauren frowned, not understanding. 'And you're both doing okay?'

'I guess so. We're not together any more.'

'Oh.' That was a surprise. He didn't look upset about it. 'What happened?'

He shrugged. 'Just didn't work. It was never ever going to be serious between us. It started as a bit of flirtatious fun and a way for me to blow off steam after a horrendous day and she was there and somehow it became a relationship for a little while.'

'I'm sorry it didn't work out.' But she was re-evaluating her choice to wear the dress now. It had never occurred to her that Oliver was *free* of Daria. Willow hadn't mentioned it. 'The girls never said.'

'They never really liked Daria, to be fair.'

Lauren smiled, recalling some of Willow's phone calls. 'I know.'

'So I never mentioned it when the relationship drifted away.'

'Is there anyone else, then? Someone new?' she teased, as if she were his best friend and not his ex-wife. She wanted to sound as if she was interested in his life, that it was just a fun conversation, but she really wanted to know. If he was with someone, that made being with him much safer. But if he was single, like her...

'No. No one. I'm concentrating on myself and my work right now.'

She nodded and tried to look sage, but inside her heart was thudding. *Oh.*

Oliver was *single*.

Single!

'What about you? How are things going with you and Mike?'

And that was when she realised that he didn't know that she was single either. Should she admit the truth or pretend that everything was fine? Deep down, she knew she couldn't lie to him. She never had and she never would. She'd always been up front about her feelings with him.

'It's over. It fizzled out some time ago.'

He frowned. 'Sorry to hear that. I thought everything was going well?'

'It was for a while. Until I found out he was having an affair.'

'Oh. That must have been awful.'

'I should have known, to be honest. He had quite the reputation on the hospital grapevine. He was an excellent surgeon but a crappy human being and the only reason the relationship went on as long as it did was because I was so busy with work I didn't notice what was happening right beneath my very nose. I felt quite the fool when I realised, because all of the signs had been there.'

She'd brushed over how incredibly embarrassed she'd felt at the time. Feeling like the whole hospital knew and that they'd all been waiting with bated breath for her to realise that Mike was not only sleeping with a redheaded radiologist, but also a blonde paediatric nurse *and* a student midwife. Clearly, he liked them young, which had never boded well for her, and when she'd asked him about what he'd ever seen in her he'd said something vaguely patronising and misogynistic about how he'd been enamoured with her because of the way she'd looked up to him as her mentor. How she'd wanted to learn from him, the way she'd hero-worshipped him. She'd made him feel good and her giving herself to him had been like the cherry on the cake.

Well, she would never hero-worship anyone again and that was why today had felt so weird, because her new boss, her new mentor, was her ex-husband. A man she had once worshipped and adored. A man she had been intimate with. A man who knew her, probably more than anyone else did! A man who, quite frankly, had known how to give her the perfect orgasm! How could she create that professional distance she needed from him so that she could continue to be the surgeon she wished to be? Their relationship had held her back once before and now that her career was on the rise she would not allow it, or their history together, to press pause on it once again.

'I'm sorry you had to go through that.'

'It was fine and it's over now. In the past.'

Like you and me.

They finished their drinks and then decided to head out to find a restaurant. Oliver said he had one in mind and as they stepped out into the cold November evening Lauren shivered slightly and wished she'd brought her big coat rather than a shoulder wrap.

Oliver noticed and shrugged off his jacket and draped it around her. 'Here.'

'No, it's fine. I don't want *you* to be cold.'

'I'm fine. Honestly.'

The warmth of his jacket around her was very pleasurable and she was most grateful for his kind gesture. It reminded her of the times he'd done it before, saying it was okay because he always felt hot. And he certainly didn't seem to mind, even though when she'd arrived earlier that evening she'd noticed him stamping his feet to keep warm. He wore only a dark shirt up top and, knowing him the way she did, she had to assume he wore no tee shirt underneath.

Maybe all that extra muscle he's grown will keep him warm?

The jacket smelt of Oliver, a familiar scent that scrambled her brain whilst it simultaneously handed her images of being wrapped around him, their bodies entwined, dizzy and breathless after sex. How she'd loved those moments afterwards, just clinging to one another, laughing and snuggling and kissing. Drunk on his scent and with memories swarming all around her, she cleared her throat, trying to ignore the familiar feeling of arousal that was awakening her senses.

'How far is the restaurant?'

'Er...just down here.' Oliver pointed down a side street to a small establishment, lit up with Christmas lights and a sign outside that said Giuseppe's.

He seemed to have no idea at all of the turmoil she was in and the second they stepped inside she slipped off the jacket and passed it back to him, relieved to be breathing in the restaurant aroma of Italian food—lots of rich tomato flavours, aromatic sauces, garlic bread and dough-balls.

'Table for two, please.'

The waiter that met them, whose name tag stated his name was Joey, led them to a candlelit table beside the window that flickered with fairy lights. The table had a glass vase in the centre, filled with tiny multicoloured baubles in red, green, gold and silver.

Oliver held out her chair for her so she could sit down. She'd forgotten what a gentleman he was, how he'd always used to do that for her whenever they'd gone out.

'Thank you.'

Joey presented them with a drinks menu and they ordered wine, which was brought to their table in a carafe, and then they began to peruse the menu.

'This looks good. I'm starving,' Lauren said.

'Me too. It's been a long day. A good day,' he added, looking at her over the top of his menu. 'Thought I'd best add that, considering my company.'

She smiled at him. 'I knew what you meant, don't worry. You know, I can't remember the last time I ate out at an Italian restaurant.'

'I can,' Oliver said with a grimace. 'It was before I met Daria and I'd decided that it was time for me to start dating again. I met this lovely woman, Maggie. Blind date, set up by one of my friends at the hospital. She seemed great until we sat down, and then she proceeded to be horrifically demanding to the waiter, and when she didn't get what she wanted she demanded to talk to the restaurant owner. I walked out halfway through her speech about whether the breadsticks were stale or not as I felt so embarrassed.'

'No!'

'I waited for her outside, told her it was probably best we didn't meet up again and wished her all the best for her future.'

Lauren laughed. 'I'm so sorry! I shouldn't laugh, but I know how you feel. I think I probably had my fair share of dating disasters too.'

'What happened to you?'

'Well, there was one guy who kept picking his nose and examining his finds whilst we tried to eat at a friend's barbecue. Then there was Kenny, who kept texting his mum throughout the meal. Oh, and let's not forget Marcus, who told me that he would order for me and then sent my plate back to the kitchen because, and I quote, "You've put way too much food on her plate."'

'Yikes.'

'And I don't even want to go into what happened when I used a dating app. Let's just say some guys ought not to think that sending me pics of their anatomy will somehow get them a date.'

He chuckled. 'Yeah, I've never quite understood that.'

'I hear you. Why can't we just go back to the days when you would send a girl you liked a mix tape? And you'd scrawl your initials in a heart and practise your new surname!' Lauren laughed, then realised she'd done exactly that with Oliver. He'd given her a mix tape. Or, rather, he'd burned a CD of songs for her—songs that he loved and thought she'd like. And she, because they'd been at university, had practised writing Lauren Shaw as a signature, convinced that the name fitted her perfectly, looked perfect with that big, dramatic S shape, and clearly convinced herself that it would be for ever.

It hadn't been. They'd lost ten years.

But maybe they could claw back their friendship, if nothing else?

They ordered their food when Joey returned to the table and Lauren couldn't help but notice how relaxed Oliver was. When they'd been younger, he'd always seemed distant, because his mind was always on other things—work, patients, clinical trials, research. There always seemed to be a million things running through his head. Now he seemed so chilled. It was the relaxed attitude of a man who had got to the place in his life where he wanted to be.

'I envy you.'

Oliver looked up, surprised. Confused. He arched an eyebrow. 'What do you mean?'

'You seem to be in a place where you're happy, career-wise. There's still a way for me to get to where you are.'

'You'll get there.'

'I know, but it will take time.'

'*I* envy *you.*'

Now it was her turn to frown and then laugh in disbelief. 'How come?'

'Because it's all still ahead of you. So much to discover and learn and build.'

'Do you wish you could have done things differently back then?'

He looked at her intently, then smiled. 'I do.'

'Such as?' She wanted to know if he regretted their past. If he regretted his decisions in any way. *Their* decisions.

'I felt that opportunities for us to talk were missed.'

Lauren bristled. 'About?' Because if he was about to start blaming her for something, then she would defend herself.

Oliver sighed. 'We both had dreams, I know we did. But we made the decision that I would work, and I did that. I held up my side of the bargain and I worked hard for us. For all of us. Me. You. The girls. And just as I thought we would have time for one another when the girls were older, that was the moment you decided to leave and walk away. I was hurting. I was lonely. I probably said things that I shouldn't have, and that made it impossible for us to be with one another in the same room, when we could have been if we'd handled it differently.'

'You're saying it's my fault?' she asked, feeling her anger rise. 'What about my feelings, huh? Yes, we agreed you'd work, but that agreement didn't include you spending so much time away from home that I felt like a single mother! You didn't even notice I was hurting! That I felt like I was being left behind so you could become a surgical bigshot. You didn't see me any more because I wasn't a part of that world, so when the chance came for me to take back what was supposed to be mine, I took it! And you can't blame me for that.'

Lauren looked away, at the other diners. They'd kept their voices low but they'd been filled with anger and resentment. How quickly old hurts had resurfaced. How quickly old arguments had returned. It couldn't be this way. She'd moved down here to work. With him. In the same hospital. They had to find a friendlier footing.

She took a steadying sip of wine. Decided to focus on something else. 'Rumour has it that you're about to become the head of the department when Phillip retires.'

He nodded. 'I'm sorry. I didn't mean for us to argue.'

'It doesn't matter.'

'It does.' He also took a fortifying sip of wine, deciding to take advantage of her change in topic of conversation. 'I've heard that rumour too. But don't believe everything you hear on the grapevine.'

'No?'

'It's nice for it to be said, it's nice that everyone agrees that I'm the natural choice, but I like my job right now. I like where I am. My routine. Becoming head of the department would take me away from Theatre. There'd be meetings and admin that I don't particularly enjoy.'

'Then hire people to take care of that for you, whilst you remain in Theatre and treat patients.'

'You think that would be possible within an already strained hospital budget?'

'Maybe.' She shrugged, but she didn't really care. Not about that, anyway.

'I do want to be head of the department. It was all I ever wanted when I first set out as a surgeon. But all that straining to reach something made me such an intense person that I didn't make enough time for anything else. You know that more than anyone.'

He was referring to when they were married, when the girls were small. All the extra hours he'd put in at work. Overtime. Extra shifts. Working weekends and holidays. How many Christmases did he miss because he kept volunteering to cover the department? It was an old thought that caused her pain.

'The only thing I get intense about now are my visits to the gym, where I have a strict workout routine. Work I want to enjoy. Time off I want to enjoy. Becoming head would mean I'd just spend that time writing reports and worrying about budgets and shift scheduling. I love Phillip. He's a great guy and an even greater surgeon. But he clocks less hours in Theatre than anyone else. He runs one clinic a month. His list is shorter because he's always in meetings. As I've got older and closer to my goal, I've begun to realise that maybe it wouldn't be the best thing for me.'

'Or you could take the role and make it your own. Run it the way you want it to be run. Delegate. Make bold new strides in what a head of department can be.' Now she was trying to be encouraging.

He smiled. 'You always had my back. Even when I didn't have yours.'

She didn't respond because at that moment their food arrived. They'd skipped starters as they always did, preferring to just have mains and desserts, as Lauren could only ever handle two courses. Oliver had chosen a hake, sweetcorn and brown crab orzo, whereas Lauren had chosen a chanterelle gnocchi with spicy sausage. The food smelt delicious and as it was placed in front of her she suddenly became aware of the rest of the restaurant—something that had slid into the background as she'd sat and talked to Oliver.

Music played in the background. Couples sitting at tables all around them were talking and laughing, clinking glasses and raising toasts. Wall sconces lit the room and in one corner a beautiful Christmas tree already stood, reminding her that the festive season was approaching and that this year she'd be able to spend it with her girls without having to worry about catching a train back to Edinburgh.

This was going to be her life now and Oliver

was going to be in it again, albeit in a different role to the one he'd always had before. It was a shame that it hadn't worked out for them because she'd always thought of him as the love of her life.

'Do you ever wonder what our lives would have been like if we'd not fallen pregnant so soon after we got together?' she asked. It was something she'd often thought about. The path not taken. What would he think? Would he think she missed him and wanted him back? Because that wasn't true! She missed him—yes, of course she did. She missed that connection. Missed knowing someone one hundred percent. Loving someone one hundred percent. But did she want him back? They were two completely different people now, despite them both being single. And their old hurts still remained, clearly.

He smiled. 'Sometimes I do, actually, yes.'

She smiled back, grateful that he hadn't looked at her curiously, but had simply agreed that he'd often thought the same thing.

'How do you think that would have looked?'

Lauren let out a sigh as she thought and her gaze rested on a couple in the far corner. They were young, about the same age that she and Oliver had been when they'd got together. They were staring at each other, obviously completely in love, loving each other's company, blissfully unaware of anyone else, because no one else mattered.

'I think that we would have had more time for ourselves. I think that I would have finished medical school at the same time as you, started work at the same time as you. Maybe got my career established *before* the babies came along. That maybe we'd have had more time together, even if that was at work.'

He nodded. 'I don't regret the girls, though. They're my greatest achievement, hands down.'

'Mine too.' She was so proud of Kayley and Willow. Of how they'd become adults in their own right. A lawyer. A doctor! They must have done something right together. One final glance at the loving couple in the corner, at the way the guy was staring into his date's eyes, smiling, one hand stretched across the table to hold hers. Funny how talking about the girls could bring them together. But why wouldn't they?

Lauren missed that. Work was great, absolutely. She'd been waiting to start her career for a very long time and she was enjoying it, but she was beginning to miss having someone to come home to. To have someone with whom she could share her day. Someone to hold her in bed at night.

Mike had never been a great cuddler. He'd never been a guy to hang around and linger.

They'd meet up, have dinner, or a drink, have sex, and then he'd be getting dressed, checking his watch, apologising for leaving so soon, explaining that he had something on. She'd felt quite lonely in that relationship, worse than when she'd been single. So it had been easy to end it, especially when all the rumours about him had turned out to be true. She refused to be used.

'Do you think Kayley will be okay? If she doesn't get pregnant, I mean? Her and Aaron are such a lovely couple. I'd hate for it to put a strain on them both.' Lauren knew something like that could be damaging for young couples.

'I think she and Aaron both have very sensible heads on their shoulders. They talk. I know they do. Aaron called me once and asked me what he could do to support her, as he knew she was really feeling it each month.'

'He's a good guy, huh?'

'He is. She married a good one.'

Lauren remembered Kayley's wedding. It had been a wonderful day, but a little bit strained for Lauren, knowing that Oliver would be there and that they were a few months free of their decree absolute. It was the first time they'd be seeing each other after splitting up and she wasn't sure how it would go, seeing him again, both of them emotional and proud of their eldest daughter. Would their old bonds of love and attraction lead them back into old habits? Weddings made people wistful. Weddings allowed people to make big mistakes when too much alcohol became involved. Most of all, Lauren had told herself not to get drunk at the feast afterwards and fall into bed with her ex-husband! Because he'd looked so good that day, she'd thought. Dressed in his top hat and tails, smelling wonderful, smiling constantly, proud and happy. They'd had to stand next to each other a lot in photographs, trying to be nice to one another so that the day didn't feel uneasy for Kayley and her new husband, and Lauren felt sure they'd managed it very well.

But there'd been that moment at the bar when she'd fetched drinks for her friends and Oliver had been standing there, cravat removed, top button undone, looking relaxed and gorgeous, and she'd felt a strong urge to drape her arm around him and pull him onto the dance floor and slow dance with him. Hold him close, rest her head upon his chest, feel the pounding of his heart and his hand in hers. Just to pretend, for a little while, at least, that the last couple of years hadn't happened.

But weddings did that to you. Made you maudlin and emotional and full of what-ifs. And she'd known she couldn't be drawn back into her ex-husband's orbit, only for them to fit into old roles of resentment and hurt. It was why she'd avoided him as much as she could after that. Organised family events so she could see the girls on their own, without him being there. It was why being with him was such a risk now.

She must have lost her sparkle for a moment because Oliver leaned in to get her attention. 'Hey. You okay?'

She smiled. 'Just remembering her wedding day.'

'Ah.' He nodded. 'Great day. She looked amazing, didn't she? When I saw her come down the stairs in her wedding dress…' He drifted off, eyes glazed with memory, and she saw briefly the approach of tears, his eyes welling up, and then he gathered himself, sniffed, laughed and took a sip of his drink.

'She did look amazing.' She wanted to reach out then. Take his hand in hers. Squeeze it. So she could show him that she knew how he felt, that she'd been incredibly proud too. That she'd been astounded at the sight of their eldest daughter coming down the stairs, so much so, she had dabbed at her own eyes with a tissue so as not to smudge her wedding make-up.

But she couldn't take his hand. Wouldn't. It was what she'd been afraid of, coming back.

There was a boundary between them now, created by their divorce and estrangement, and she needed to respect that. But it was hard. She knew this man inside out. Knew that he could be emotional and appreciated physicality. His love language was physical touch, as was hers, and so it felt incredibly limiting not to be able to do that.

'Look at us!' He smiled, trying to lessen the tension of the moment. 'Getting all maudlin. That's not what tonight should be about. We should be celebrating!'

She smiled. Nodded. 'We should.'

'You're back. You're doing amazingly. We're all healthy and well. What more could we ask for?'

Plenty, she thought, but did not say.

'We should have fun tonight. Eat this lovely food. Listen to the Christmas music that's playing far too early.' He gestured to the speakers set high above them that were already playing festive songs. 'We should be enjoying each other's company. I want this to be good between us, Lauren. I know we're divorced and we have history, but we should make the effort to enjoy being with each other because we share so much even though we chose to be apart, and there's no reason why we can't do that.'

Lauren smiled, raised her glass. 'Agreed.'

He clinked his glass to hers. 'To a shared future.'

'A shared future.'

* * *

They enjoyed a lovely meal at Giuseppe's. After the initial wariness at going out to dinner with his ex-wife, Oliver was glad that they'd both agreed to just enjoy each other's company and the conversation became easy and natural after their little hiccup. He often found he had to remind himself that they were divorced and that they hadn't just gone back in time.

He loved sitting opposite her, sharing a meal. It was nice. More than nice. They'd not often had the time to enjoy each other's company when they'd been married. He'd always been working—overtime shifts, covering when they were short of staff, grindingly hard work, learning as much as he could, as quickly as he could. He'd found a mentor in Phillip and stuck to him and other visiting surgeons to absorb as much information as he was able, so that he could be the best doctor that he could be and all that time Lauren had stayed at home and taken care of their daughters. He'd felt guilty about it. Not being with them. Missing milestones. She'd done an excellent job without him, but in that work grind they had lost opportunities in which they could have been together and he'd missed so much. Family meals. Working during birthday parties. Taking extra shifts at Christmas because of the better pay. Being on call.

Had it all been worth it? Losing his wife, failing at his marriage had hit him hard. It had been so easy to work so hard, knowing that Lauren would always be there if he needed her. And then when she wasn't? When she'd gone and he had no one to come home to? He wondered what it had all been about. He'd so looked forward to the years when they would have time together, but it had never happened. He'd been so focused on their future he'd never noticed the present.

When had he last taken his wife out for a meal? One of her birthdays? A wedding anniversary? In the restaurant he'd asked her if she could remember.

'Our twelfth wedding anniversary.'

'Really?'

'Yep. We went to that sushi place, where the dishes went around on that conveyor belt thing.'

'That's right! I remember now.'

'And you left halfway through, because you were on call and the hospital messaged you as one of your patients had to go back into surgery.'

'Really?'

He didn't remember that part, but maybe he'd blanked it out because he knew he'd let her down.

As they walked through the square, lit with premature Christmas lights, he marvelled at her strength. She'd put up with so much. No wonder she had finally walked away and claimed back her life for herself.

'Thank you, Lauren.'

'What for?'

'The sacrifices you made when we were married. I'm not sure I fully appreciated what you gave up for me.'

She shook her head. 'I loved my family. I loved being a mum.'

'But you wanted to be a surgeon.'

'Yes. I put up with a lot to hold off on that dream. Most especially from my parents.'

He remembered. Lauren's parents had never had a great relationship with their daughter, but they'd had high hopes for her and had pushed her academically so that she would excel in life. The dark looks he'd received from them as if it was just his fault that she'd got pregnant, not once but twice, would live in his memory for ever.

'How are they?'

'The same.'

'Wondering why you're not head of the hospital yet?'

'Probably wondering why I'm not the Health Secretary yet.' She laughed. 'Whatever I do, it's never enough. I thought they'd be proud of me finally going after my dream and becoming a surgeon, but now all they say is, *Isn't it a bit late for all that now?*'

'Ouch.'

'Yeah.'

They looked across the square. A large Christmas display was going up, Santa on his sledge, led by his flying reindeer, rising up into the sky. Beneath them, a house, complete with a Christmas tree, and outside, a snowman.

'There were so many things I wanted to do with my life, but never got the chance.'

'What else did you want to do?'

She stopped to turn and look at him, consider him. 'That.' She pointed at the display.

He was puzzled. What did she mean? 'What?'

'It's silly but… I always wanted us to build a snowman as a family and yet we never did that. Not in all the years we were together.'

He frowned. 'You did. I've seen pictures of the ones that you and the girls built.'

'Me and the girls, yes. But *you* were never there. You never built a snowman with us. You were never around for snowball fights. You were never there when we would go back inside, all wet and cold, and we'd warm up with hot chocolate and wriggling our toes in front of the fire. We missed you, Oliver. The girls and I, we missed you. A part of us was always missing.'

She sounded so wistful, so hurt. He'd had no idea.

'You never said.'

'Would you have listened? Would you have stayed away from work?'

He thought about it. He would now, that was for sure. But back then? When he was a different Oliver to who he was now?

'No. I would have gone to work. Said we needed the money.'

'We did need the money. But the girls also needed their father. And I needed my husband. Just for those moments. To help us make memories. A lot of our memories don't have you in them. There are almost no photos of you— have you noticed that?'

He felt bad. Guilty. He'd felt bad at the time, but he felt doubly so now. He'd thought he was doing the right thing for his family. It had been drilled into him that fathers provided for their families, no matter what. That you worked. That if you were lucky enough to be offered overtime, then you took it.

'I thought I was doing the right thing.'

'I know. And I appreciated your sacrifice, as you appreciated mine. It just would have been nice, on occasion, to have felt like *we* came first.'

Oliver nodded, knowing he could never make that mistake again. The urge to defend himself was strong but…he knew he was just as much to blame for his marriage breakdown as Lauren was. Her frustrations had often come out

as anger and the arguments that they'd had towards the end…

Neither of them had ever dealt with blame in
the way that they should have.

'You know, if Kayley ever does get pregnant
and you become a grandfather, you'll want to be
around. You won't want to miss any of it.'

She was right. He wouldn't. 'Grandfather.
That word comes out of nowhere, doesn't it?
You can accept yourself as an adult. A husband.
A father. But then you hear the word grandfather
and it all suddenly sounds so terrifying. Are we
really getting that old?'

She laughed. 'Well, you might be.'

He loved her laughter. Her smile.

'Don't speak too soon. Grandma.'

She gave him a playful shove and now it was
his time to laugh.

With her. Something that they should have
made more time to do, all those years ago.

CHAPTER SEVEN

LAUREN WAS AN hour into her breast reconstruction surgery on Callie Mackenzie when she became aware that Oliver had entered Theatre.

She felt a warm glow grow within her at seeing him once again. Ever since their meal out together a week or so ago they'd been getting along just brilliantly at work and, as ever, she was keen to show him her abilities as a surgeon.

'How's this going?' he asked.

'Yeah, good. Callie was one of my first patients here and keen to have this done urgently and so she chose to go privately. I feel we've come full circle. It will be good to see her going home feeling like everything is back to normal.'

'You're doing body tissue reconstruction?'

'My patient preferred it to an implant.'

He nodded. 'Are you choosing to perform a TRAM or DIEP flap?' A TRAM flap was tissue used from the lower abdomen, specifically from the traverse rectus abdominal muscle, whereas a DIEP flap was tissue used from the deep inferior epigastric perforator. It spared the muscle and had fewer complications than TRAM flaps.

'DIEP.'

'How many have you performed before?'

She looked at him over her mask. 'Three.'

'Solo?'

'Two assisted. One solo.'

'So, this is your second?'

'I suppose.'

'Want help?'

'Don't you have your own patients?'

'Nothing until midday.'

She'd wanted to do this alone, to show that she could do it. She was confident about this and had felt sure that she would stride out of Theatre with a good outcome. She wanted to be able to ring her parents and tell them what she'd done today. Alone. By herself, with no one's help. Hear them say, *Well done*. Plus, she was a surgeon and surgeons could be territorial.

'I'm okay. But you could observe, if you want.' She hoped that he would take that the right way and understand. Surely he'd understand, being a surgeon himself. Or would he take it as a rebuke? She needed him to see, also, that she was capable, not a medical student or junior any more.

'Then I'll observe.'

She sucked in a breath to calm herself as he stood there and watched her perform the surgery.

Why did he unnerve her so? She was doing just fine until he came into Theatre and everything was going well.

'BP is dropping,' said the anaesthetist. 'Hanging another unit.'

Callie had bled quite a bit, but she'd got the bleeding under control and hopefully that would assist the blood pressure with the extra unit going in. But the procedure was going well and she'd already had a doctor from Plastics pop his head in to see how she was doing. She felt confident, if only people would leave her alone to get on with it.

'Anything from Kayley yet?' she asked him, to distract him from the intense gaze he was giving to her surgical field.

'No. Nothing. You?'

'No.'

'Willow's not heard anything either. She told me last night.'

'You saw Willow last night?'

'Not for dinner or anything. We just happened to bump into one another as we were leaving the hospital. And I literally mean bumped into one another. She tripped over one of those fake presents under the Christmas tree in Reception.'

Lauren smiled. 'She okay?'

'Yeah, it was just a little trip. She didn't see it because she was texting on her phone.'

'Sounds like Willow.'

He laughed. 'It does. I often wonder if she's been surgically attached to it.'

'We could always perform an amputation.'

She looked up at him and smiled. She liked this Oliver she was seeing these days. He was so different from the intense, driven Oliver she had known in their formative years. That Oliver had always had a frown, had always seemed stressed. This Oliver, this more mature Oliver, seemed much more relaxed. More calm. But she guessed that was what happened when you were confident in your own ability, had been in the same job for years and had reached the top of your tree.

'Suture, please.'

The theatre nurse passed her the suture and needle and she began to close the incision. Lauren was tired, but also not tired. It was a strange thing, theatre. You could stand in there for hours, concentrating, working, saving a life, or rebuilding one, and you could go in there absolutely knackered, but somehow standing there, with a life in your hands, made all those aches and pains disappear. Surgery was a great focus for the mind and body. It was afterwards, when the adrenaline level dropped, that you'd feel it.

'Done. Would you like to take a look?' she

asked Oliver, pleased with her work, with the result, with the neatness of her stitches.

Oliver stepped forward to examine her surgery.

She found herself looking at him, holding her breath, as she waited for his praise, and she realised how much she wanted it from him. Just as much as she wanted it from her parents. Praise was something that had always been sadly lacking in her home when she was growing up and so it was something that she always sought out, hungry for it. She hated that in herself sometimes, but she just couldn't help it.

'Looks good.'

That was it? She'd expected ebullient praise, over-the-moon stuff! And all she'd got was, *Looks good.*

She'd have to take it, she guessed. It was better than criticism. And she also had to remember that, as a senior surgeon, it was also Oliver's job to help raise the baby surgeons. Giving them too much praise at the beginning might make them cocky, and a cocky, overconfident surgeon could sometimes be a danger. And she was still a baby, compared to him. He'd been doing this for decades now and she was still in her first five years of being a surgeon.

Your education as a surgeon never stopped. You were always learning. Always being allowed to do more and more complicated surgeries. And with time, knowledge and procedures changed too, as surgery adapted itself with new technologies and assistive machines. The field of surgery was an ever-changing beast and a surgeon had to be prepared to change with it.

She was beaming as she scrubbed out. He could see the pride in her face, the sense of accomplishment, and he was happy for her.

She was glowing, in fact. He'd not seen her this radiant since they'd been at medical school together and they'd sit and chat about their dreams for the future. They'd both dreamed of working in reconstructive surgery, admired the way lives and quality of life could be changed. They'd both wanted to be head of their department. Oliver had dreamed of leading the way by doing surgeries that would be broadcast to other hospitals, so that other surgeons could watch his brand-new pioneering techniques that he would have come up with himself. He'd dreamt of the Shaw Method, not knowing back then what it might be, but hoping that one day it would exist. Lauren had dreamed of being head of a department and lecturing around the world and taking under her wing groups of doctors that she would personally mentor and educate.

They'd sit in the quad at university together

and dream big, laughing and imagining the future together as they ate lunch, or quizzed each other for tests. They were great days. Days that he missed.

But he could see that same glow in her eyes now and he suddenly felt wistful, wishing that Lauren could have had it all back then. That she could have followed her dream at the same time as him. That she could be where he was today, professionally, because maybe they would have stayed together. Maybe there wouldn't be this distance between them, a distance he'd always hated and felt unable to overcome.

But if she'd had her dream then they most probably wouldn't have had Kayley or Willow and he loved his girls more than anything.

Life was strange—difficult—with many winding roads.

If they were together, what would he be doing right now? Kissing her and holding her, congratulating her on a surgery well done? Would they sneak a moment in a linen cupboard on occasion, like some couples in this hospital? Or would they both have been so busy with their respective work that even then they wouldn't have had enough time for one another and would have drifted apart as their careers took off?

Maybe we were always doomed to drift apart?

'I'll let you get on, then,' he said, feeling a little blue.

'Wait, Oliver!' She dried her hands on paper towels and threw them in the bin, then unhooked the safety pin that held her rings from her top. She slid them back onto her fingers. She still wore her wedding ring, he'd noticed. He'd noticed it that night they went out for dinner. 'Are you okay?'

He nodded and forced a smile. 'I am. I'm happy for you, Lauren. You should call your parents. Tell them what you did today. Tell them that you changed a woman's life.' He gave her a nod, another smile and left the scrub room.

Once upon a time, Lauren had changed *his* life. With her choice of a fluffy purple pen. The way she'd tucked her hair behind her ear in a lecture. The way she'd smiled when he'd asked her out. The day she'd told him she was pregnant.

Everything had changed the day he'd noticed her.

He'd been so determined when he started medical school that he wouldn't let anything distract him from his studies. From his goal. He was the first in his family to go to medical school. The first to go to university at all! He didn't want to screw it up, his one chance to do well. To escape the endless grind of work that his own father had been consumed by.

But he'd been helpless at the sight of her. The way her blonde hair had fallen over her face. The way she'd licked her lips when she was concentrating. He'd been drawn to her like a moth to a flame, telling himself he would only introduce himself, say hi, make a new friend and then walk away.

But it had been impossible to walk away from Lauren. And his biggest mistake was believing that she would find it impossible to walk away from him.

He'd thought that they would be together for ever.

But he'd been wrong.

Through his own mistakes.

She had walked away to pursue the dreams that she'd put on hold for him. For their girls. Now she was working towards her dreams and he was determined he would make her happy.

He would help her excel now.

And he would stand back and watch her star rise. If that meant standing in a darkened corner whilst she stood in the spotlight, tucking her blonde hair behind her ear, whilst the medical world watched her being an amazing, pioneering surgeon, then so be it.

He would watch.

He would help push her.

And he would clap the loudest.

CHAPTER EIGHT

LAUREN WAS ENJOYING a cup of strong coffee on a break when she was beeped. She looked down at her phone and saw she was being paged by Oliver.

Call me ASAP

She wondered what it could be about. Kayley? Willow? A patient?

The last couple of days, there had been speculation in the reconstructive surgery posse that Oliver was planning a huge surgery, something that would put the Great Southern and their department firmly on the map, but no one knew exactly what it was. Nor had she had the chance to talk to him about it, because he'd always been holed up in his office or on video calls and could not be disturbed. It had almost begun to feel as if they were married again, with Oliver being too busy to spend time with her. But that had been okay. She was used to not being with him any more, though since they'd met again at this new job she'd actually been really enjoying his company.

So she dialled the number and he picked up instantly.

'Lauren?'

'Hey. You paged. What's up? Are the girls okay?'

'As far as I know. Whereabouts are you?'

'Er… Level B. Overlooking the gardens, which I have to say are starting to look quite sorry for themselves.'

'Can you come up to my office?'

'Sure. When?'

'Now. There's someone special I'd like you to meet.'

'Oh. Okay.'

For some reason, her stomach turned and she felt oddly concerned that when she got up there Oliver would introduce her to a new romantic interest. The idea of him with someone else was quite disturbing, strangely, now that they were working together. Being in Edinburgh and hearing he was with someone had been easier than seeing it in the flesh. Perhaps he was trying to be respectful to her? To disclose the relationship to her first, before he went public with it with everyone else?

She dumped her coffee, which now left a sour

taste in her mouth, in the closest bin and took the stairs, needing to run off some pent-up energy that was now fizzing through her veins with nerves.

As she got to his office she could hear a woman's laughter inside and her heart sank.

Buck up, Lauren. Be happy for him.

She had no idea why she was feeling this way. He wasn't hers any more! But because they were getting on so well with one another lately, the way he'd look at her when he thought she wasn't looking, the way they'd laugh together, she'd kind of figured that…

No, don't be stupid. Nothing is ever going to happen.

Lauren rapped her knuckles on the door and the laughter stopped. She felt sick, knew she needed to gather herself to hear this news. Show that it didn't bother her. She wanted Oliver to be happy. He deserved happiness, of course he did. He was a good guy. A great guy.

'Come in!'

She sucked in a deep breath, squared her shoulders and forced a smile before pushing the door open, and then stopped in her tracks as she realized she'd misjudged the situation completely.

Oliver was sitting behind his desk, smiling, and opposite him were two people, a guy in his mid-forties, holding a blue manila folder that was thick with reports and, beside him, a woman of indeterminate age, who was missing half of her face. Her nose was gone, her cheeks were red with vicious scarring, one corner of her mouth twisted up, exposing her teeth.

'Lauren, come in. Close the door. I'd like to introduce you to Paul Slack. He works with a charity that supports bomb victims and this is Mina Barakzai, our new patient.'

Lauren closed the door quickly. So this wasn't about a new girlfriend—this was about work. She moved forward, shook both Paul's and Mina's hands. 'Nice to meet you.'

'Take a seat, Lauren.' He waited for her to do so. 'Paul and I have been working on and off together over the last few years. When he can, he brings over patients who need extensive maxillofacial or body reconstruction and today we have the wonderful Mina here, who is going to receive a partial face transplant.'

A partial face transplant? Lauren had never seen one of those done, though she'd heard that Oliver had been involved with two before.

'I consult with surgeons in and around the UK and bring together, when we can, a team of surgeons, max fax, reconstructive, plastic, to change an individual's life and we've been consulting on Mina's case for a while. We were never quite sure if it was going to be a go, but now that we have a perfect donor match she's scheduled for surgery next week and I'd like to bring you in on the team.'

Lauren stared at him in shock. She couldn't believe it. A partial face transplant was huge. She couldn't believe that he would value her work like this, bring her in on something that juniors didn't normally get a look in. Usually, they would observe or watch on video as something momentous like this was completed. To actually be in the room...? But she knew she couldn't react with surprise with the patient sitting right next to her. This woman was going to go through an immense change, physically, mentally and emotionally, and she would want to see confidence in her team. So, instead, she pasted a serene smile upon her face.

'That's wonderful. Thank you!'

'I have all of Mina's files and records here and I will go over them with you to bring you up to speed, but what I'd like you to do first is consult with the donor team and the family. It's important you get to know everyone involved.'

Of course. A face transplant couldn't happen without someone donating theirs. Somewhere, a family was hurting, grieving, but generous enough to consent to this. That made them terribly brave and courageous in Lauren's book.

'Absolutely. Just let me know what you need me to do.'

'I've emailed you their details. If you could go over their files before you go to meet with the family?'

'Of course.' She stood again, turned to face Paul and Mina. 'It was a pleasure to meet you.' She shook both their hands again and made for the door, before turning and smiling at Oliver once again before she left. It was a thank you. A sincere thank you. Being involved in a case like this would be momentous, not only for the patients involved, but also for her career.

She couldn't wait to get started. Heading over to one of their consoles, she punched in her access details and brought up the files that Oliver had sent. They were extensive, hundreds of pages long. But she flipped through the files until she reached the donor information. They were here, at this hospital.

Anjuli Maguire was a perfect blood and immunological match for Mina. Aesthetically, she was also a good match for skin colour, tone, gender, ethnicity and even the size of her face matched Mina's. Anjuli had been taken into A&E at another London hospital a few days ago, after being involved in a road traffic accident between a car and an HGV and had suffered irreversible injuries. Her husband, Leo, had consented to the donation after confirming his wife was an organ donor.

Leo and Anjuli had been placed in a side room. Leo sat beside his wife, face pale and blank as he held her hand in his. Anjuli was attached to a ventilator, but had been declared brain dead.

Lauren slipped into the room and stood in respectful silence for a moment, waiting for Leo to notice she was there. He didn't look at her, but began speaking first.

'Is it time?'

'No, Mr Maguire, not yet. I've just come down to introduce myself to you. I'm Dr Shaw. I'll be one of the reconstructive surgeons helping to work on your wife.' She sat down in the plastic chair next to Anjuli's bed and gazed at the donor. She looked serene, at peace. There were no visible marks to her face from the crash. Her records stated that not only had she suffered irreparable damage to her upper spine that would have paralysed Anjuli for life, but she'd also suffered what was called an internal decapitation.

Leo frowned. 'Wasn't the other doctor called Shaw?'

She nodded softly. 'Oliver. Yes. But no relation.' It was just easier to say than to explain. This man did not need to hear the complicated situation they were in. She placed her files down on the cabinet gently. 'Leo, would you mind if I ask you a few questions about your wife?'

He nodded and sighed. 'Sure. But I don't know what else I could tell you that you haven't already tested for. You doctors have taken every conceivable bit of blood or tissue that you've needed for your testing.'

He was probably right.

'Tell me about Anjuli. What kind of woman was she?'

Leo looked at her, surprised. 'You want to *know* her?'

'I do. She's a person and I think it's important and, if you don't mind, with your permission, of course, I'd like to be able to tell the recipient about the kind of woman Anjuli was. Confidentially, obviously.'

He probably thought that, as doctors, they viewed his wife as a piece of meat now, something to be quartered and shared, her organs her only value. But Lauren had never looked at patients like that. Every person was an individual, with a family, a history. With desires and dreams. Loves.

Leo smiled. 'She was wonderful. I couldn't have asked for a better woman to be by my side. Loving. Giving. Generous. She signed up for one of those donor cards as soon as she came to England. She believed in it, you see. She had a nephew, back in Afghanistan, who'd received a bone marrow transplant that saved his life. She wanted to do that for someone.'

'It says in her files that she's also donating other tissues.'

'Her corneas. Her skin. She would have wanted to donate her organs if she could, but they were damaged in the accident.'

'I'm so sorry. I know this must be hard.'

'This bit's easy. It's what she wanted. She would give the shirt off her back. *This*...this isn't the bit that's hard. What's hard is how I treated her. How I took her for granted. I just expected she'd be at home, waiting for me each day, and I'd stopped...' He gulped and wiped at his eyes. 'I'd stopped noticing her. Thought I could carry on every day, without having to make an effort, you know? The day she died, we...we'd argued about it. She told me I made her feel unimportant, like she was a nobody, and that someone at her work was willing to treat her like the queen she ought to be.'

He broke down then and Lauren handed him a tissue from a box to wipe his eyes and waited for him to calm down.

'She stormed out, took the car, and all I could think of was to show her that I wasn't bothered. My pride stopped me from going after her. I thought she'd gone somewhere to sulk, maybe to one of her friends' houses. And then the police turned up at my door. Our last words to each other were spoken in anger and I'm going to have to live with that. So of course she'd do this. It's why I'm letting you do this. Because it's what she wanted, and I never gave her what she wanted.'

'I'm sorry.'

She didn't want to give him any false platitudes, tell him that his wife knew he loved her and that maybe, rather than focusing on those last few moments they'd shared, perhaps he ought to focus on all the good ones. Because that wouldn't help, not really. Humans were curious creatures and she knew that Leo would focus more on those last few hours of his marriage than he would on all the other years when it had been good. Those last few minutes together would colour his memories, taint them. Make him regret. Make him punish himself.

She sat talking with him for some time, learning about the woman that Anjuli was, and he gave her permission to talk to Mina about her, if she ever asked.

Lauren left him to spend his last few hours with her. The machines would keep her body alive until the operation to help Mina. But she couldn't stop thinking about Leo. About how he could only focus on what had gone wrong in his relationship with his wife and couldn't focus at all on any of the good parts. Their falling in love. Their wedding day. Waking up in the morning with her. Cuddling with her during a movie. Sharing a joke. Making a home together.

It made her wonder if she'd done the same thing towards the end of her marriage and afterwards. Why did she never focus on that fresh-faced Oliver who had tracked her down after a lecture and made her blush? The Oliver who had once given her his coat when an unexpected rainstorm had threatened to drench her? The Oliver who had cradled their daughters in his arms, seconds after their births, and gazed at her with such love and adoration and told her she was amazing? He'd been there for her during the two births of their daughters, had hated leaving her home alone to go to work because he'd wanted to hold them in his arms.

She smiled at such memories.

How easy it was to look at the complaints, to focus on the negative, when they'd actually had so much positive stuff too. And this extra time she was getting with him now, learning from him, knowing him in a different way, not as his wife but as a colleague, a friend… She should enjoy it, enjoy her time with him.

Because time was a gift that some people didn't get to have. Accidents happened. Disease happened. HGVs coming out of nowhere happened.

She and Oliver could forge something new now, something different. Maybe even something deeper?

With a renewed mindset she strode towards the ward to do her ward round, feeling positive and excited about life.

CHAPTER NINE

LAUREN WAS JUST finishing for the day when she got paged to the hospital canteen. She frowned as she looked at the details, checking to make sure she was reading them right. *The canteen?*

Her legs ached, her back ached. And she'd been looking forward to going to the swimming pool tonight and getting in a few lengths to stretch out and work out the knots that were forming in her back. Maybe even twenty minutes in the sauna would have been nice.

But, clearly, she was needed, though for the life of her she couldn't think why a reconstructive surgeon might be needed at the canteen, so therefore this had to be a social thing. Oliver? Willow?

Yawning, she covered her mouth and rolled her shoulders, trying to work out the kinks in her muscles as the lift transported her down to the floor she needed. The doors pinged and slid open and then she was striding towards the canteen, thinking about all the delicious food she could eat tonight. Maybe treat herself to a take-away for a change? She'd not had a good biryani for a while. That might be nice.

She was so busy thinking about food that at first she didn't recognise who she was seeing. It had been a long time since she'd seen them all standing together, but there they were!

'Kayley! Aaron! Oh, my gosh!' Her eldest daughter, Kayley, and her husband, Aaron, were there, with Willow and Oliver. Their whole family together, with the exception of Willow's fi-ancé. 'What are you doing here? You look amazing. That holiday must have done you so much good!'

She kissed her daughter's soft cheek and gave her a big squeeze, feeling grateful that they had come to see her. It felt so good to feel her in her arms once again. She'd been so worried about Kayley of late, not having had any contact with her, and since her talk with Leo that afternoon she'd been trying to think about her last con-versation with her eldest and what they'd said. In fact, it had become a little bit of an obsession as she'd worked that afternoon, thinking of her last words with her daughter. She'd told her she was worried about her and that she could always come and talk to her about anything. Kayley, as usual, had been blue and evasive and she had so much to worry about, with trying for a baby, she'd not wanted Kayley to feel bad.

But now she could put that right. Lauren could put that right with everyone. She wanted her last words with everyone to be kind ones. Words of love. It was important.

'It was amazing. I can't wait to tell you all about it. But Aaron and I have felt so guilty at being AWOL for so long we thought we'd come here and see you all together. We figured it was our best chance to get you all in the same room at the same time!' She laughed.

Lauren laughed too. She was probably right. They were all so busy with their respective jobs and careers that finding a time when they were all available was always going to be difficult.

'Have you come straight from the airport?'

Kayley shook her head. 'No, we came home yesterday. But we were here at the hospital earlier today and figured we'd gather you all together.'

'Here at the hospital?' Something had to be wrong. 'Were you sick whilst you were away?'

'No, not sick. Look, why don't we all sit down? I'd love something to drink.'

'What can I get you?' Aaron asked everyone.

They all ordered hot drinks, with the exception of Kayley, who ordered an orange juice.

They chatted socially for a little while, with

Kayley telling them all about how beautiful Croatia was, the coastal towns, the small villages, the architecture. She showed them all photos on her phone.

Lauren thought she looked happy—happier than she'd been in a long, long time—and it was so nice to see. The shadow of infertility had hovered over her daughter's head for far too long. Maybe she'd accepted it. Maybe they'd both come to the conclusion that if it was going to happen, then it would. They just had to relax a bit more about it. Lauren had often heard that once the pressure was off, many couples would go on to conceive naturally and that sometimes it was all the stress and worry that prevented conception.

Whatever it was, it was nice to see. Kayley and Aaron's holiday had certainly done them the world of good.

As Aaron arrived back with the drinks she noticed how happy and relaxed he looked too.

'Croatia sounds wonderful and, by the looks of the pair of you, maybe we all ought to go there and enjoy the restorative powers of the place,' Lauren joked.

'Maybe!' Kayley laughed.

It had been such a long time since any of them had heard that sound and it gladdened Lauren's heart. She glanced at Oliver and caught him watching her. He was smiling too and, just for a brief moment, she could believe that they were together again. That they were a family again. How many years had it been since they'd all been together like this?

Too long.

And it felt good, so good. She felt in that moment that she could cry with gratitude.

'You mentioned you were at the hospital earlier, Kayley. Is everything okay?'

Kayley glanced at Aaron and reached for his hand. She was beaming. 'Actually, yes, I'm more than okay. We both are.'

'Then why were you here?' asked Oliver.

'Well, we have some news. News that we've both known for some time, actually. I'm…no—*we* are pregnant.'

Lauren gasped, hands covering her mouth in shock. 'Really? Oh, that's wonderful!' Now she did begin to cry tears of happiness as she reached over to throw her arms around Kayley.

Everyone got emotional, even Willow. They'd all been part of Kayley's struggle to get pregnant. They'd all witnessed her depression, her obsession with her monthly cycle—hoping and praying every month that there would be no sign of it. Hoping that each cramp didn't mean the onset of her period but was instead her womb changing because of an embryo. That each time she felt like her breasts were painful or swollen it was because they were changing due to pregnancy. That each time she suddenly felt a craving for a particular food it was because she was carrying a child and not just hungry. They'd all hoped along with her. They'd all dreamed. They'd all lost when they'd wanted to believe in something so much and it had crashed and burned around their ears, and they'd all been stoic and brave as they'd tried to support Kayley and not mention their own sadness.

Kayley pulled out a string of ultrasound photos. 'This is why we were here today.'

Lauren examined a picture, absorbing the details of a clearly shaped baby in the womb. She could see a head, a spine, arms and legs, a little baby curled up, safe and secure. Then she noticed the details. Each scan picture was identified with patient details and measurements of the baby.

'This says the baby is measuring at twelve weeks and three days.'

Kayley smiled. 'Yes, I'm sorry we never told any of you before, but we knew we were pregnant at six weeks. But after the last miscarriage we didn't dare tell anyone. I was so convinced it might happen again, I wanted to wait until after the twelve-week scan, which we had today.

Baby's fine. I'm fine. Strong heartbeat. I think we're going to be okay with this one.'

'Oh, Kayley!' Lauren was so happy her tears fell anew as she gazed at the ultrasound of her first grandchild.

Oliver reached out to hold her hand across the table and she was grateful for it. Grateful for his strength. He knew how much they'd both hoped for this one day.

'When's the due date?'

'May twelfth.'

'A May baby. Oh, honey, I'm so happy for you both! We all are!'

'You don't mind that we hid it all from you?'

'Of course not!'

'We just wanted to hold onto it for ourselves, in case of…you know.'

'We do know. And you did absolutely the right thing.'

'We knew we'd be scared in the run-up to the scan, so we booked some time away. We could afford it and thought it would be a good thing to do, and if the baby stuck then it might be our last holiday away as just a twosome.'

'We understand, honey. You don't have to explain yourselves to us.'

'I'm going to be an aunt.' Willow smiled dreamily.

Lauren and Oliver smiled at her.

'Have you thought of any names?'

'We didn't dare. Not until today.'

'You can start planning now.'

'I don't think I'll ever truly relax until he or she is in my arms.'

Lauren laughed. 'And even then you won't, not really. Being a mum means you worry about them constantly. Even when they're fully grown.' She reached up to tuck Kayley's hair behind her ear.

'Thanks, Mum.'

They stayed chatting for a while, then Aaron glanced at his watch. 'We need to get going if we're going to catch my parents and tell them the news too,' he said.

'Oh, my goodness! Of course! We've been hogging you both,' said Lauren. 'Do forgive us, it's just that we've not seen you both for such a while.'

Aaron grinned. 'It's understandable. Don't worry.'

They waved the happy couple away and Lauren sighed as Oliver's arm came around her for a quick squeeze.

'It's great news, isn't it?' she said dreamily, already imagining all the baby clothes she could buy.

'Fabulous news. We should celebrate. This deserves a celebration, a family one. What should we all do?' Oliver glanced at Willow, hoping she'd have some ideas.

'Don't look at me. I've got plans tonight.'

'Oh, anything nice?'

'I'm getting me some culture tonight. I'm off to the theatre to see a musical.' She checked her phone. 'Actually, I've got to dash or I'll be late.' She leaned in, gave them both a peck on the cheek. 'You'll have to wet the baby's head without me!' Willow smiled and headed off.

Oliver turned to her. 'I guess it's just you and me. Unless you're busy too?'

'I'm not busy and I'd love to celebrate the baby with you. We should, actually. Seeing as we're both now going to be grandparents.'

The word settled in her mind.

Grandparents!

It was actually going to happen.

She felt tears of joy threaten again, but she'd shed enough tears.

'Let's do something amazing. Something festive! What do you think? You and I used to love Christmas.'

'Well, we don't have any snow, so we can't build a snowman, but I do know somewhere with ice.'

'I don't want to go to a bar, Oliver.'

'I didn't mean a bar. I meant a rink.'

* * *

Their very first date, he'd taken her to an indoor skating rink. It had been vast, echoey and cold and over the scent of the ice was the distinct smell of old sweat from the legions of hockey players that used it for game nights. But they'd been able to dismiss that because they'd been having fun together. Lauren was like a baby deer on ice, much worse than him, but they'd got through it with laughter and fun and it had totally taken away the awkwardness of touching each other, because every time Lauren had threatened to fall over she had grabbed him and held onto him for dear life.

Now, as they bent over to tie on their skates for this beautiful outdoor rink that was situated in Hanover Square, he was reminded of it.

'I hope you're an expert by now,' he joked.

Lauren looked at him with a raised eyebrow. 'Are you kidding me? The last time I went skating was the first time I went skating.'

'You've not done it since?'

'Well, let's see…no. I was too busy raising two children and then becoming a doctor to find time to whizz around on the ice. How about you? Are you about to show off your triple axel?'

'I can do triples in my sleep.'

'Really?'

He laughed. 'No! I haven't been skating either.

The most I've slid around on ice since is when I've done so in my car, and I don't think that's quite the same thing.'

He saw relief on her face that they would both be bad at this and he liked making her feel that way.

Oliver reached out his hand. 'Come on. Let's go show everyone how this is done.'

She took it. 'Show them what, exactly? How to fall on their bum?'

'Maybe not that part.'

'I just want to get out of this without a visit to A&E, okay? Remember, I'm at higher risk for osteoporosis now I've hit menopause.' Her smile was infectious.

'I'll take good care of you.'

'Thank you.'

But then, just before they stepped out onto the ice, he turned and tried to look solemn.

'But if we *do* end up in A&E I'll ask the ambulance crew to take us somewhere other than the Great Southern. I'd hate for our colleagues to show up and take photos of our bruised coccyxes.'

'Very good point.' She laughed, taking his hand as he stepped out onto the ice and held onto the side with his other.

Had ice always been this slippery? He grimaced slightly, trying to look confident for

Lauren's sake as she nervously stepped out and instantly began to wobble. One foot went out from under her and she lunged for him, grabbing onto both his arms, laughing.

'Seriously? Oliver, maybe this is a bad idea. I really want to do that face transplant with you, but neither of us is going to be able to do it if we've got broken wrists by the end of this!'

They were both steady again. As long as they didn't try to move.

'If you fall, remember to roll.'

'I don't want to fall.'

'Come on, we can do this!'

Christmas music was playing out over the speakers and in the centre of the rink, protected by barriers, was a ginormous Christmas tree, beautifully decorated with stars and tinsel and baubles and guarded by four Nutcracker soldiers in their finest gold and yellow uniforms. Around the rink were stalls selling all types of food and drink, from roasted chestnuts, which smelled delicious, through to hot chocolates, burgers, loaded fries and even ice cream!

Slowly but surely, both Lauren and Oliver gained their balance. It took a lot of holding onto the side and holding onto each other. A lot of laughing, squealing and shrieking at near falls, but the bit he liked the most was the way that she held onto him. As if she needed him.

Having her this close again, after all those years, did something to his insides that he'd never expected. His body yearned for her, the familiarity of her. He'd loved this woman, had been in love with her, and deep down he would always love her. She was the mother of his children. She was the one who would make him feel good after a difficult day at the hospital. She was the one who would soothe him when he lost a patient after they threw a clot that caused a catastrophic stroke. She was the one who'd held the fort at home, who'd held him in bed, and he missed those soft curves. He missed the way she felt against him, and having her hold onto him like this now made all sorts of thoughts and feelings ricochet around his brain and body.

It was as if he'd travelled back in time and this was their first date again, only this time they *knew* each other. There was no awkwardness. He could just revel in being with her, watching her beautiful smile, hearing her beautiful laughter. He laughed alongside her. How long had it been since he'd felt so carefree, so relaxed, a part of something good?

When Lauren finally got her balance and was able to let go of the side, he tried it too and they skated hesitantly, slowly, holding onto each other's hands, trying to not get bumped by anyone else, and he was so proud of them as they finally began to get their skating legs and could go a little faster.

'Look at us go!' Lauren called.

'We put all these youngsters to shame. Let's show them how it's done!'

And they did, for a little while. If all they were showing was how to skate badly, leaning forward much too far, arms waving wildly at their sides. But they were having fun and they were happy and that was what mattered more than anything else.

But, obviously, pride came before a fall and it wasn't long before one of them—they couldn't agree who afterwards—tried to go too fast and pulled both of them down onto the ice with a thump.

They cackled with laughter, cheeks red, as they tried to help each other up into a standing position again. They weren't near the edge, so had nothing to hold onto except each other, and because they were laughing so much all their strength seemed to have left their legs and they almost found it impossible to stand up without slipping over, again and again. But eventually, somehow, they staggered back to their feet and wobbled to the side to rest and get their breath back and then they pulled themselves along to the side opening of the rink and disembarked, removing their skates, putting normal shoes back on, and then they bought themselves two giant mugs of hot chocolate topped with whipped cream, tiny marshmallows and chocolate flakes.

The drink tasted great and it was the perfect accompaniment, warming them up, giving them back some much-needed energy in the form of refined sugar, and there was something wonderful about sitting next to the rink, sipping at a hot chocolate as Christmas songs played over the speakers and skaters whizzed around on the ice.

'That was such fun, Oliver, thank you,' Lauren said after he'd walked her back to her flat.

They stood outside and he could see the lovely glow of her cheeks in the lamplight from the street. Her eyes gleamed, she looked happy and it made him feel good to know that he had been a part of that. When had they last laughed and enjoyed each other's company like that when they'd been married? Too long ago. They had both allowed work and life to get in the way and they'd been so busy being Mum and Dad that they'd forgotten to be husband and wife.

'It was. We should do it again some time.'

She smiled, nodded. 'We should.'

'Maybe next time we go skating we'll have a little grandbaby. We can get them to push one of those penguin things the other kids were using.'

Another nod.

But then a thought penetrated his head. Here

they were, having had fun together, and already he was talking about the next time involving their grandchild. He would spoil any grandkids he had, clearly, he would, but did he have to bring them up right now? He'd just thought about how they'd let their own kids get in the way of them being a couple—would he make the same mistakes with grandkids too? Because, right now, he felt as if they were the old Oliver and Lauren. The ones who were together before they had kids. Shouldn't they enjoy this? Shouldn't he focus all of his attention right now on Lauren?

'Or, you know, we could go there again on our own. That's important too.'

He must have said the right thing because she laughed and smiled, nodded again.

'Maybe we could.'

'I enjoyed being with you tonight.'

'I enjoyed it too.'

He looked at her, wondering if this time when he kissed her goodnight, he should still kiss her on the cheek. Because what he really wanted to do was kiss her on the lips.

'Would you like to come in for a nightcap? I've got a single malt Scotch that I think you'd really like.'

She'd remembered his favourite tipple. And hell, yes! Because he wasn't ready to say goodbye yet.

'That would be great, thanks.'

Lauren got her keys from her bag and unlocked the door and led him up to her flat.

It was smaller than his, but neat and perfect, just like Lauren. She'd filled it with comfy sofas, throws, pillows, soft lighting. There was a floor-to-ceiling bookcase, jam-packed with titles, and he remembered how much she liked to read. How sometimes on a morning before he had work, when he came out of the shower, he would find her reading in bed, glasses on, concentrating deeply as she lost herself in a love story. Lauren adored love stories. In particular, she loved a book that could make her cry. One time he'd found her sobbing as she sat there, turning the last few pages of her book, and he'd cradled her and said, *'Hey, don't read it if it makes you this upset.'*

But she had pushed him away so she could carry on reading and cried, *'No, that's what makes it so good!'*

He'd never quite understood that. Never understood how, after the book was finished, she'd smile and wipe her eyes dry and sniff and sit there looking dazed and say, *'That was amazing.'* He'd never experienced that with a book.

'You've got a nice place.'

'Thanks. I'm still kind of unpacking. Don't

look in the spare room—all the boxes are still in there.'

He smiled. When they'd lived together, she'd always had a room, a small storage space, where she'd hidden things, so that if visitors ever came to the house they wouldn't see mess. He used to call it her hiding spot.

Some things didn't change.

'Here you go. It's from a distillery called Bavenny. The guy that owned it brought me a bottle once for looking after his wife in hospital when I was a junior.'

Oliver took the glass and decided to raise a toast. 'To Kayley and Aaron and our first grandchild.'

She smiled and clinked her glass against his. 'Kayley and Aaron and our first grandchild.'

He took a sip and raised his eyebrows in surprise. It was an amazing Scotch whisky, rich, strong notes flavoured with malt and honey. 'That's good.'

His gaze was caught then by a photo on the wall of Lauren and the two girls. Kayley and Willow were young, maybe three and four years old, and they were on a beach. Lauren sat behind them, holding them close as the wind whipped their hair in all directions. The girls were laughing and it looked like Willow had the remains of an ice cream cone dripping over her fingers.

'I don't remember this.'

'You wouldn't. You weren't there.'

He frowned. 'I wasn't?'

'It was our trip to Cornwall. You didn't go because you had a big case you were prepping for and so the girls and I went alone.'

'That happened a lot, huh?' he asked, already knowing the answer.

Lauren nodded. 'I didn't want the girls to miss out, so we went by ourselves. We were used to it. I found this picture when I was packing up in Edinburgh to come down here. It was in the back of a photo album that I'd forgotten about and I really liked it.'

'Any photos of me in there? All of us together, as a family?'

'One or two. Mostly at your parents' house.'

He nodded. 'I'm sorry that I was absent.'

And he meant it. But he'd been trying to build his career quickly, so that they would be comfortable financially. Having two young babies and a wife to support as a junior doctor had been terrifying, but he'd thought that, with dedication and a little bit of sacrifice, he would earn more money the more shifts he worked. That his skills would improve more quickly than other doctors if he put in the hours and, besides, hospitals had plenty of beds. He could sleep at work and get there early, before anyone else, make connections, study under the best.

'You did what you thought was right for your family.'

'But I never asked you if it was.'

Lauren looked down at the ground. 'I don't want to blame you, Oliver, because you had a great work ethic. You were dedicated, knew you had to make it work for us if I was staying at home and not earning myself. And, you know, maybe I was at fault too. I never showed you how much I felt down at missing out on my career, putting it on hold. I blamed you a lot back then, held resentment tightly to me, like a shield. You made sacrifices too, but I couldn't see that. Time with our girls was so precious and you missed it. But I never once thought about how that must be hurting *you* too. I should never have shut you out so much.'

And in that moment he almost cried. Because she saw him. She realised the pain he'd been in too. He might have been working for them, but he'd also known just how much he was sacrificing by not being there. At the time it had felt like the right decision, but now, seeing how much it still hurt…the repercussions, all these years later…divorced. The sacrifice didn't seem worth it. So what if they'd not had a lot of money? They would have got by. They would have found a way. Lots of people did. Why had he felt so driven to work so hard, and effectively make his wife feel like a single parent?

He would never make such a mistake again, and he knew in his heart that when his first grandchild came along he would not miss out on his or her upbringing. He would be present. He would be a fun grandpa. He would take them out and spend quality time with them, spoil them rotten, because he'd missed his own kids growing up. He wouldn't miss it again.

Oliver put down his tumbler of whisky and reached for Lauren's hand.

Surprised, she set down her own glass and looked up into his eyes. She was so beautiful, even now. If anything, her beauty had grown. The flecks of grey in her hair, the extra laughter lines around her eyes. She looked stunning.

'I want to make a promise to you. To you and the girls and the grandchild to come.'

She smiled, her eyes gleaming.

'I will be present for this. I will not be absent. I will be there for them and for you. Whatever you need of me, I'll be there for you.'

'Oliver, you don't have to—'

'I do. Being with you all at the hospital this evening, sitting at that table in the canteen, felt incredible, all of us together like that, and it made me realise just what I'd missed before.

All those times we could have had but I lost, because I put working first. Because I put money first, before my family. Being with you tonight at the rink…that was…so much fun. I couldn't remember being that happy for a long time, and you made me feel that way.'

He couldn't help but notice the way her blue eyes softened, the way her smile widened, the way she caressed his hand in her own. How had he ever allowed himself to lose her? How had he ever been so proud that he had let her walk away?

'I've missed us. I've missed this. And tonight, watching you laugh, seeing your smile, it reminded me of how good we used to be together.'

'Oliver…' She raised his hand to her lips and kissed it. 'I had fun tonight too. Tonight was how it should have been between us. When we first got together, it was fun and surprising. You'd take me places and make me close my eyes and guess where we were. We were spontaneous. We were fun. I've missed that.'

'Do you think we could ever find that again?' he asked, knowing it was a dangerous question, but still thinking intensely about how her lips had felt pressed against his skin a moment ago.

Lauren smiled. 'Well, let's see, shall we?'

And she raised herself on tiptoe and pulled him in close for a kiss. A soft kiss. A loving kiss.

A familiar kiss, but, despite its familiarity, it was exciting and strange and his body responded in the only way it could when he was with Lauren and he took her in his arms and decided to forget the world.

CHAPTER TEN

SHE'D WANTED TO kiss him all evening. Something strange had happened at the ice-skating rink. Oliver had gone from being her ex-husband and senior work colleague to someone she wanted to be with. Her feelings for him that she had been keeping contained had spilled over with every fall on the ice, with every time he'd caught her, steadied her, laughed with her. His body had felt so familiar and yet, oh, so different at the same time. She'd felt hard muscle, she'd sensed strength, he smelled delicious, and when they'd both fallen flat on their faces and she'd fallen into his arms and practically landed on top of him...well, she could have kissed him there. On the ice. In the middle of the rink. But the way she'd been feeling then, that kiss would have led to her wanting more, and it would not have been appropriate to do all the things she'd been thinking about doing to Oliver since she'd begun working for him.

He was easy to be around. She'd felt relaxed,

happy. The news about becoming grandparents had been wonderful. Knowing that Kayley was actually all right and was finally pregnant had lifted a huge weight off her shoulders that had been there for weeks. There'd been no need to worry. Kayley and Aaron were fine. Willow was doing well, and she and Oliver? Well, she'd wanted to celebrate that. Why not, after all? They'd done something right. They'd raised two beautiful, strong, independent women who were living their own lives and living their own dreams and so was Lauren.

Oliver was the closest person she had to a friend down here now, the one who knew her the most, so of course it was easy to be with him. And as he slowly removed her clothes, as she slowly removed his, she began to feel like the Lauren she'd been when they'd first met. When they'd first slept with one another.

Somehow, they made their way into the bedroom. As much as Lauren liked the idea of their lovemaking being so passionate he could make love to her up against a wall, she also knew that at her age her back and hips would not thank her tomorrow! She knew from experience that she wanted a soft place to fall, a comfortable place to lie, so that she could fully enjoy all the wonderful sensations that Oliver was causing.

Of course he knew how to touch her. He remembered what she liked and so she did not have to teach him or guide him with her soft moans of pleasure. He not only knew where to touch her, but he was also finding new places. Unexpected places. Gentle kisses on the underside of her breasts. A tongue gently flicking at her wrists. And so much more. She lay there, gasping, as his tongue and mouth explored her, as if he was making sure he missed nothing of her, exploring her, re-familiarising himself with her. And all the time she felt his hard body above her, his muscles, his hardness brushing over her, leaving little trails of kisses.

She wanted to close her eyes and just revel in what Oliver was making her feel, but she also wanted to see him, watch him, enjoy him. Lauren pulled him to her, eager to feel him inside her, but he kept teasing her, brushing her, licking, kissing, the flicks of his tongue hot and tantalising. The small groans of pleasure whenever their lips met, the way he whispered her name…

And then he rolled over, pulled her on top of him, and now she pressed his hands above his head as she decided to play his game. She would tease him, provoke him, explore him with her hands and mouth. His body was rock-hard and a feast for the eyes and she could not believe he was hers. Her tongue trailed his nipples, his abs. She moved lower and teased more, felt him thrust against her in urgency and need, which made her smile and feel her power as she ran her tongue around the tip of him, heard him groan as she took him in her mouth and he clutched at her head, fingers grasping her hair as he thrust towards her again.

She held back, flicked her tongue against him again, before she climbed his body and gave them both what they wanted.

It was the hottest night of her life. Had sex between them ever been this way before? Maybe. But pregnancy and years as an exhausted mother had erased those memories. Perhaps it had always been this great in those early days before the girls had come along. She liked to think that maybe they had been. Or maybe they'd both just learned a thing or two in their years apart. Maybe maturity and satisfaction in their vocations had given them both the ability to just relax now. Maybe before they'd always tried too hard because they were younger and they'd thought they had to be a certain way with one another and it had never had the intimacy that tonight seemed to have.

It was the same, but it was different. Vastly different. Lauren felt more confident, more assured in her power as a sexual being. Plus, there was no risk here of pregnancy. This was fun. Pure fun. Pure lust. Pure need. And there was a freedom in that that she'd never felt before and she was determined to enjoy it to the full.

When she woke the next morning, sated and aching, she had a huge smile on her face. She lay in Oliver's arms and it felt so good. As if she was back where she belonged. Cosy. Snug.

Outside, she could hear the wind blowing, trees thrashing, the gale whistling around her building like a storm was brewing. But for her it felt calm. Peaceful. Right. Oliver was the big spoon and his arms were wrapped around her and she laid her hands upon his and then began stroking his arm as she thought about last night.

Being with Oliver again... She'd never imagined that this might happen between them. She'd thought that maybe they'd moved so far apart in the last decade that it was never even a consideration. She'd thought he was still with Daria! Kayley and Willow hadn't told her anything different, so to find out he was single...

They'd been working well together, getting over the initial discomfort after meeting again, of being his subordinate, worrying over Kayley. But then the good news. The pregnancy. The baby! They were going to be grandparents! A happy day indeed, and that happiness had brought them together again.

The skating at Hanover Square had been hi-

larious and bonding and fun. Their walk back to
her flat had been quiet, contemplative, intimate.
She had felt his protection as they'd walked
through the London streets, his reassuring presence by her side, in a way that felt strange, but
oddly pleasing. Showing him her flat, the look
in his eyes when he'd apologised for being absent. He'd looked so pained and she'd not wanted
him to feel that way. All of that was in the past
and it had never just been his fault that the marriage failed.

Lauren had made choices too that had contrib-
uted to its failure. Giving up her career to be a
stay-at-home mother. She'd wanted to do that.
Had felt, at the time, that it was the right thing
to do. She'd not wanted her children to be raised
by nannies and pre-school clubs and after-school
clubs, never seeing their mum or their dad because they were always at work, because that
was the way she'd been raised. Her father had
worked all hours, her mother too. They were
consummate professionals, always besuited, always busy, always so focused on paperwork or
on the phone, even when they were at home, that
Lauren had barely felt noticed, had felt like she
was a burden to them. A mistake that they had
to make allowances for and work around.

That wasn't how she'd wanted her children
to feel. She'd wanted to raise them in a loving

family and so she'd prioritised her family over her career. And had continued to prioritise them until the girls had gone off to university, and then she had sat back and wondered what was next for her and what had happened to her marriage.

It wasn't just his fault. She'd never thought about how their situation had affected Oliver. She'd felt pressure to prove to her parents that she was doing well and she'd wanted, desperately, to make them proud of her. Neither of them had been impressed at her staying home and playing mum and housewife. Her mother had often called her and had asked, exasperated, if being just a mother all by itself was fulfilling, that surely she wanted more.

And so she'd gone looking for more, had returned to her initial dream of becoming a surgeon, like Oliver, and she'd pushed for it, and her education, her training, had torn wide open the gap between her and Oliver and it had seemed simpler to just separate. And then divorce.

It had been an incredibly painful decision. She'd never for one moment thought that her marriage would end that way, or in any way, but it had.

And now here she was, right back where she'd begun, and though it ought to feel frightening, or even vaguely embarrassing, to be back in her ex-husband's arms after a night of the most wonderful lovemaking they'd ever experienced, it didn't feel that way at all.

It felt good.

She felt content.

If she were a cat, she'd be purring.

But, like before, Lauren was an early riser. She was always the lark, Oliver the owl. And though she loved being here in his arms, she was also starving and desperate for the loo, reality impinging on her perfect moment! If this were a movie or a book, she thought, she'd get to lie there for a while, maybe even wake Oliver with an arousing touch, or turn to face him and stroke his face, and though she yearned to do all of these things, the siren call of the bathroom proved too much.

Very carefully, she slid out of his arms and grabbed her robe, tying it at the waist. Looking at Oliver briefly, she smiled. He looked good in her bed. Those muscular arms, that broad back, his flat abs...

Bathroom!

She hurried to relieve herself, sighing with release and unable to stop herself from smiling.

In the kitchen, she began making coffee, then remembered that she was absolutely ravenous and opened the fridge. She saw bacon, sausages, eggs. Perfect! She would make a full English cooked breakfast. He used to love those. She had bread too, so she could fry it, or toast it. There was a solitary tomato on its last legs, she could use that too. Pity there were no mushrooms, but in the freezer she found a half empty packet of hash browns.

She hoped she wasn't making too much noise as she pottered about, sipping her coffee, hoping to make a nice breakfast to wake Oliver up with. Maybe they could climb back into bed afterwards, snuggle. She turned the radio on low and quietly sang to some tunes as she cooked and she was so absorbed and so happy in what she was doing—when had she last cooked a meal for someone other than herself?—that she was surprised when Oliver's arms came from around her back and she laughed as he nuzzled into her neck and kissed her.

'Good morning,' he said.

'Good morning.'

Of course she'd worried. Worried about what this morning would look like. It could have been embarrassing. It could have been awkward. She might even have woken up to find Oliver gone, having crept away to do the walk of shame in the middle of the night. But no. He'd stayed in her bed, with her tightly wrapped in his arms, and it had been perfect, but she'd been prepared for the embarrassed excuses, maybe even an apology: *I'm sorry, this should never have happened.*

But she'd hoped that it wouldn't end that way and here he was, snuggling into her, all warm and cosy from her bed, and he seemed to have no regrets about last night, which was good because right now neither did she.

'I hope I didn't wake you,' she said, putting the pan lid over the sausages to stop them from spitting fat everywhere.

He turned her to face him. 'I reached out for you and you weren't there. That woke me.'

She smiled. 'Sorry. I was starving and for some weird reason I'd worked up quite an appetite.'

He kissed her on the lips. Slowly. Pleasurably. Making everything tingle from the tips of her toes to the top of her head.

'Want to work it up even more?'

Lauren laughed. 'I'm in the middle of cooking!'

'Turn it down. Or off. It'll keep for ten minutes.'

'Ten minutes? That long?'

He nibbled on her lip as his hands smoothed over her bottom and pulled her up close against his erection.

'Maybe fifteen.'

How could she resist? She turned in his arms

to switch off the cooker—better to be safe than sorry—then giggled as he took her hand and pulled her back to the bedroom, and he showed her exactly how hungry *he* was.

It had been the perfect way to start the morning, back in Lauren's arms, and after they'd finished, they'd squeezed into her tiny shower cubicle and soaped each other up and washed each other down and realised that if they carried on like this then neither of them would make it into work on time!

He'd driven them both in, promising that he would give her a lift home in the evening, but now that he was seeing patients, in between prepping for the surgery on Anjuli, he wondered if taking her home was all he wanted to do.

They'd had such fun together last night at the ice rink and just being able to be with her, spend time with her and enjoy just being them again, had been the most wonderful thing he'd ever experienced. He'd felt like himself again. Like he'd rediscovered the Oliver he used to be, before ambition and needing money to provide for two small daughters and a wife had taken over.

It wasn't about feeling young again, though last night and this morning had made him realise that age really was just a number. In their fifties he and Lauren might be, but they'd stayed up all night, enjoying each other's bodies like two teenagers, and when he'd woken even more hungry for her this morning... Well, he'd certainly scratched that itch too.

'So we started Mina on the immunosuppressive drugs?' Oliver was chairing a meeting with all of the surgeons who would be working on Mina's case of a partial face transplant.

Dr Bartlett nodded. 'Yes.'

'And she's tolerating those?'

'No problems reported. She seems in good spirits. A little anxious, but that's to be expected.'

'And Garrett, you're sure she's okay to go ahead from your perspective?' Dr Garrett Green was a clinical psychologist.

'I'm happy to give my approval. I've spoken to Mina at length over the last few months. We've generally met once a fortnight to discuss the surgery and what it might feel like to wake up and see a vastly different face in the mirror and she understands all that she might go through, the effect it might have on her mental wellbeing, as well as her physical and emotional health.'

'Good. And the physio team?'

David from the physio team gave a thumbs-up. 'We've gone over the facial and neck exercises that she'll need to do after the surgery and she seems to fully understand the work she'll need to put in, once you guys have done your bit.'

His gaze naturally fell to Lauren, who sat at the back of the room as she was not a primary surgeon on this case. She would only be observing, maybe assisting if she was lucky. The soft smile of encouragement she gave him made him feel great.

'And her family? Her personal support team?'

'Her family is coming over today from Afghanistan. Her mother and an aunt, I believe.'

Oliver nodded. Everything seemed ready. The surgery had got the green light and though he should be nervous, he felt excited. He felt ready. As if he could tackle anything the world threw at him at this point.

'Okay. You all know what to do. Off you go.'

The medical team dispersed, until only Oliver and Lauren were left in the room.

'Impressive,' she said, smiling. 'But then you always were confident in everything that you do.'

'As long as I know that what I'm doing is for the right reasons.'

'Giving this woman a new face…it's mind-blowing. She must be very strong. I can't imagine not seeing myself when I look in the mirror. Imagine seeing a different face. With freckles or blemishes that you never had before. The donor face has a small beauty spot on the chin, did you know that?'

He nodded. He did know. He'd examined the donor, Anjuli, already. 'And a small scar on the cheek. Barely noticeable.'

'Mina will look at that scar in the years to come and wonder what caused it.'

'Are you okay?'

She nodded. 'I am. You? No regrets?'

He smiled. 'No regrets.'

'Good.'

'You know, I think that you and I should seize the day. Let's not think too hard about us and just enjoy ourselves and do things that are fun. Things that we never got to do before. We should go out tonight, after work.'

She smiled and nodded. 'No regrets and fun? What's not to like about that?'

'I'll meet you in the foyer at six p.m.?'

She glanced around, made sure no one was around to see, before she went up on tiptoe and kissed him on the lips. 'I'll see you there.'

CHAPTER ELEVEN

'HAVE YOU HEARD?'

'Heard what?' Oliver was busy writing up a patient's notes when the charge nurse, John, sat down beside him.

'Your friend Dylan.'

'Dr Harper, you mean?'

He smiled. 'That's the one.'

'I've heard nothing. Why?' He was slightly relieved that the gossip wasn't about himself.

'Well, you know that new neuro, the pregnant one? Size of a house?'

Oliver smiled. 'Is that the medical terminology you use all the time?'

'The one in her third trimester, then?'

He meant Poppy, Dr Poppy Evans. He'd stood behind her once in the queue for food. They'd not talked much, but she seemed nice.

'I do know of her, yes.'

'Apparently, it might be his baby.'

Oliver stopped what he was doing. '*Dylan's* baby? Are you *sure*?'

'It's what I've heard.' The charge nurse leaned in even closer. 'Apparently, she went to a clinic to get pregnant and there was a mix-up with the sperm and they used his sample, rather than the guy's she was meant to use, so he's the baby daddy!'

Oliver frowned, remembering Dylan telling him years ago about donating sperm to help his twin brother and his wife to have a child, and how some of the sperm would be left in the clinic, in case they wanted another child later down the line. So it was possible that this piece of hot hospital gossip could be true.

I wonder how Dylan's feeling about this. Poor guy. What a mix-up.

'We shouldn't pay attention to hospital gossip, John.'

'No, no. Absolutely not.' John made a zipping motion over his lips. 'But…er…you're friends with Dr Harper. Has he said anything about it to you or…'

Oliver raised his eyebrows. 'I thought you weren't going to gossip? Didn't you make it your New Year's resolution at the beginning of this year?'

John laughed. 'Who still sticks to their resolutions by December? Come on, it's end of January, at best.'

Oliver smiled. 'My lips are sealed.'

But no, Dylan hadn't mentioned it, and if it were true he supposed Dylan would need a friend, someone to talk to. Dylan wasn't the type of guy to do commitment. But a baby on the horizon? That must have him feeling some intense emotions. He made a mental note to call him.

'I want my patient in bed two on hourly obs; can you make sure that gets put down in her chart?'

'Sure.'

'And Mr Burton in bed eight has requested extra pain meds. I've written a script for him, but he has quite the addictive history so only give them to him if you feel he is in need.'

'Will do. You're on top of things. Looking snazzy. Got a hot date tonight?'

Oliver smiled. 'If I did, do you think I'd tell you all about it?'

'Oh, God, I hope so!'

Oliver laughed and wished him goodnight and signed out of the computer. He checked his watch. Ten to six. He was finishing on time and he couldn't wait to pick up Lauren and head on out. He had a festive date all planned, determined to give her as much Christmas fun as she could stand, especially since he'd missed out on doing all of this sort of stuff in the past.

Last night with her and this morning had been

heaven-sent. Dylan Harper might be about to navigate the early days of fatherhood, but Oliver was an old pro and he knew now how important it was not to let yourself focus only on one thing. Providing for your children and their future was one thing, but maintaining a relationship with your partner and still treating them like a romantic interest was just as important. Both he and Lauren had not done that. He'd devoted himself to being a provider only. She had devoted herself to being a mother. They'd stopped dating one another. They'd stopped seeing each other as lovers. They'd stopped having fun together.

And he was determined, with this second chance, to put that right.

'Where are we going?'

'It's a surprise.'

Oliver was being weirdly secretive as he drove them through the London streets. The car was lovely and warm in contrast to the freezing fog outside, but it made the outdoors look beautiful, all those Christmas lights hazy and blurry. Lauren gazed out at shoppers, laden with bags or clutching hot drinks in takeaway cups, or standing by food stalls and filling their tummies with festive delights. It reminded her of how hungry she was and she wondered if Oliver was taking her out for food. A meal out somewhere would be nice.

'Are we going out to eat?'

'We are, but that's the second place on our agenda.'

'What's the first?'

'This.' Oliver swung into a parking space and she looked out of the window at a vast building that looked like a warehouse, but had a huge sign on the outside that read 'Real Snow!'

She laughed. 'What is this?'

'Believe it or not, it's an indoor ski centre where you can ski or snowboard or even…' he made a drum-roll noise '…it's a place where you can build snowmen.'

'You're kidding!' She felt excitement bubble up through her.

'I am not. I've scheduled us a half hour skiing and half an hour in the snow pit—what do you say?'

Her smile was so broad, she thought it might split her face. 'I say I'm in!' She couldn't quite believe it. Skiing? Snowman-building? That was one of her dreams for sure and she'd told him about it ages ago and he'd remembered! Which meant he cared. He wanted her dreams to come true.

Why could they not have been like this when they were younger? He'd been so good about her decision to put her dreams to one side to focus on the girls and then off he'd gone to follow his own. There had been moments, she could admit, when she'd felt jealous of him. Angry with him. As if her dreams were not as important as his. And sometimes, when he came home from the hospital with stories of everything going on, the patients he'd seen, the surgeries he'd performed, she'd tried her very hardest to smile and be happy for him, when all she'd wanted to do was tap out and swap places and let him stay at home, so she could go out and talk to adults and be a grown-up and perform surgeries.

Only she hadn't. She'd kept that rare anger and jealousy to herself and told no one. Not Oliver, not even her parents. She'd felt ashamed of it, because raising the girls had also been her dream. She'd wanted to be at home for them, she'd wanted them to feel loved, that they weren't a burden, and she felt that she had achieved that. All the same, her dreams had been put on hold. As if they weren't as important as Oliver's. It was silly and illogical because she knew they had discussed it. He had asked her if she was all right with being a stay-at-home mum and she'd told him she was.

But still…she often wondered where she'd be right now, if she'd taken a different path. Would she be like Oliver, heading up a team to perform a partial face transplant? Or still just assisting, feeling lucky if she got to hold a retractor?

Lauren tried to push all of these thoughts aside. Regrets had to stay in the past now. She could do nothing about them and she refused to let them spoil her enjoyment of today. Oliver was giving her one of her dreams—to build a snowman with him—and build a snowman she would!

The ski centre provided snowsuits, boots and skis and, because neither of them had skied before, they were taken to a baby slope and shown the basic steps before they attempted to ski down a small slope that was only a few metres long. Oliver fell over straight away, which had her rolling around with laughter, and from his place on the floor he grabbed a handful of snow and threw it at her in fun. Lauren helped him to his feet and then it was her turn and it turned out she was quite the natural!

She didn't fall once, but glided slowly and in control down the slope before she could side step back up and come down, over and over again. Eventually, Oliver stopped falling and improved control on his slowing down when he reached the bottom, but before they could feel brave enough about trying the next slope up their lesson was over and they shed themselves of the skis and headed on over to the snow pit.

This was a large expanse filled with snow crystals, where people were building snowmen and having snowball fights, or making snow angels, and everywhere she looked she saw happy, smiling faces as all around them Christmas songs played over the speakers.

She couldn't remember being this happy ever, and to share this moment with Oliver was wonderful, as if it was meant to be, having him by her side. She'd missed him, over the years. The divorce had been the right thing to do at the time and she'd always thought she'd feel an element of freedom by moving to Edinburgh, away from them all, so that she could focus on her education and training, but she'd felt so alone and so far away.

Her weekly video calls with Kayley and Willow had been nice, but it had never been the same as actually seeing them in person. She'd wanted to be like Oliver in those early days together. She'd wanted to be able to come home to tell someone about all the exciting things she'd seen that day, the first time she'd done a new suture technique, the first time she'd led a surgery, but when she came home there was no one to talk to. Her working family had become her only family, and so when Mike had started taking an interest in her…well, it had probably been easier than it should have been to believe he'd actually liked her and wanted something more than just fun and a sexual fling. She should have known better. She should have listened and paid attention to the gossip about him, but she'd felt so lonely, she was desperate for someone to show that they cared. And for a while he'd acted as if he did.

'So how do you want to do this?' Oliver asked.

'Wait, you've never made a snowman?'

'Probably not since I was six. It may be hard for you to believe, but snowman-building is not something I've been practising as much as surgery.'

'Okay. Well, I guess one of us makes a body and the other one makes a head?'

'Which do you want to do?'

'I'll take the head?' She figured it would be quicker and with Oliver being bigger and stronger, he could manhandle the snowman's body.

They got to rolling the snow, pleased with how well it clumped and stuck to itself, so that making the snowman was easy. They rolled and rolled, swiped up armfuls of loose snow and packed it down onto their growing lumps. Lauren spent some time trying to refine hers by smoothing out the roundness of the head, then decided to make a tiny snowball and smooth it onto the snowman's face for a nose. Then Oliver lifted the head onto the body he had made.

'We need eyes and a mouth.'

But they didn't have anything they could use, so Oliver took off his scarf and wrapped it around the snowman's neck and told Lauren they should take a picture before their time ran out. The half hour had passed by way too quickly and he mumbled something about wishing he'd booked an hour in the snow pit.

A friendly fellow snowman-builder offered to take their picture for them and so Lauren found herself standing behind the snowman, hugging Oliver with a big grin on her face, as their photo was taken on Oliver's phone. Looking at the picture afterwards made her smile widen even more.

'Looks great! Will you send me a copy?'

'Sure!'

She glanced at the time. 'What do we do with him? Leave him here? Knock him down?'

'I'd feel sad to do that.'

'Let's leave him here. It's his home, after all.'

They waved goodbye to their snowman and headed back outside into the biting cold and quickly hurried over to Oliver's car to turn on the heater to get warm. As she held her fingers over the warming air vents, she turned to Oliver.

'Thank you for that. I loved it. I appreciate you making one of my dreams come true.'

'Maybe we should come again and bring the girls? Do it as a family?'

She smiled, but they weren't a family. Not any more. Not technically.

'Maybe we should just keep it between us? Don't want the girls getting any ideas about what's going on here.'

'We're just having fun. Nothing to report,' he confirmed.

'Well, they may not see it like that and, besides, Kayley's pregnant. I'm not sure I'd want her to get knocked over or slip over right now.'

'True.'

She didn't want to feel hurt by his comment that they were only having fun and there was nothing to report between them, even though she knew he was right and she had been the one to say that she didn't want the girls getting any wrong ideas. Because the thing was, Lauren was getting ideas. Lauren was dreaming about what might be between them and if she was wrong—which she probably was, as Oliver had said there was nothing to report except fun—she didn't want to be hurt by it.

Plenty of divorced couples got back together for sex, right? It was probably natural and happened a lot more than most people would care to admit to themselves. And though she might secretly dream of what it would feel like to get back together with Oliver, surely there was too much water under the bridge now? They'd changed. They were different. The only reason they were spending this much time together was because…

Well, she wasn't sure, exactly. Comfort played a part. Familiarity, probably. Hidden feelings? Regrets? Attraction was still there for her, very much so! But there was something else, something she didn't want to admit to, and that was maybe, despite their divorce, despite deciding that ending their marriage had been the best thing, there was the sneaking feeling that she still loved him and always would. He was the father of her children and he had been in her life for a very long time, and here they were, back together again, both single, the responsibilities that had once weighed them down were now gone, so why shouldn't they have their fun? Maybe it would be easier this way. Maybe it would be simpler. A fling, no strings attached.

'So, what's next?' she asked.

'Food. I'm starving. Building a snowman takes it out of you.'

'Where do you want to go?'

'I know the perfect place.' Oliver started the engine.

She was happy to be led by him, happy to let him decide where they should go. She trusted him, knew he would find someplace nice, somewhere festive. It was nice to just sit back and relax and let someone else do the organising, the choosing.

As they drove through |London she listened to the Christmas songs on the radio, singing along with Oliver as they drove past businesses and homes all lit up with their trees in the window, their lights outside. She saw girls, all dressed up to the nines, tottering along the road in their high heels and sequined dresses with no coats and remembered the days when she'd done the same and wouldn't have been seen dead wearing a winter coat. Now, she was happy she was snug and warm in her thick puffer jacket, woolly hat and gloves. Glad of the occasional hot flush that ran riot through her body.

At first, she'd hated the signs of menopause, hated that it meant a portion of her life was over now and she was moving into a new phase. But just lately she'd been proud of hitting menopause. It meant she'd reached an age that some people never got the chance to reach. She'd seen too many lives lost much too early during her time working in the hospital and she'd begun to appreciate how precious life was. How every second mattered. Not being able to bear children any more didn't mean she had no purpose in life. Her wrinkles and lines told a story of a life well lived, of a history. And she had two grown daughters and an ex-husband to prove it!

And soon she would be a grandma. A *grandma!* And that was precious and perfect and an amazing gift that she would cherish. A baby to spoil, a grandson or a granddaughter, and she and Oliver would move again into another phase and that was fine. She had no idea what it would be like, but already she had hopes and dreams. She felt optimistic about the future. With Kayley's pregnancy, moving back down here, being with Oliver, it just seemed like everything was moving in the right direction and long might it last!

Oliver pulled to a halt in a side street, bought a ticket to place inside the car so they didn't get fined, and then led her to a stall near the London Eye.

'What's this?'

'The finest turkey Christmas dinner you'll ever taste in your life.'

She raised an eyebrow. 'That's some promise.'

'Try it. You'll see.'

Lauren went and sat on a bench whilst Oliver joined the long queue, and listened to a busker singing *Silent Night* to a backing track of mournful guitar and piano. The singer, a young woman, had a beautiful voice and there was a group of people standing around her, watching and listening, one or two sending their children forward to place coins or notes in her empty guitar case that lay on the floor.

After a few minutes Oliver arrived holding two steaming parcels, proffering one to her.

She gasped in amazement, salivating instantly at the Christmas wrap. It was a large Yorkshire pudding, overflowing with turkey, cranberries, stuffing, mini crispy roast potatoes, baby vegetables and smothered in a thick, aromatic gravy.

'Oh, wow!'

'Wait till you taste it.'

Lauren wanted to savour every mouthful, to delight in every bite. But she was so hungry and the wrap itself was so delicious and she ate it so fast that, before she knew it, she was licking her fingers and making sure she had got every crumb that had fallen into the bottom of the foil wrap that had been keeping it warm on such a cold winter's night.

'You inhaled that,' Oliver said, his eyes smiling.

'I was starving and I've never tasted anything like that in my life, not from a stall. How did you find this place?'

'Confession—I didn't. Willow did and she brought me last year. Knowing your love for Christmas dinner, I figured it would be a hit.'

'Well, it was. Do they finish it off with Christmas pudding, drowning in brandy sauce?'

He laughed. 'I'm not sure. Want me to check?'

'No, I was only joking. I don't think I could eat another bite until New Year's.'

'Want to walk it off for a bit?'

Lauren looked along the river, as far as she could see, lit up with fairy lights. It could have been a photograph, a scene for a Christmas card. Who wouldn't want to stay and linger for a bit?

'Sure.'

It seemed colder along the riverfront, but Lauren didn't mind. She was in a celebratory bubble.

'So…*grandparents*. Are we ready for that, do you think?' she asked him.

'I think so. How about you?'

'I knew it would happen one day. As soon as Kayley and Aaron got married, I knew this part was coming. For a while there, I wondered if it would, what with the miscarriage and then the trying that they did, but yes, I think I'm ready. When is it too early to start buying Baby-gros?' she said, laughing.

'She's made it through the first trimester.'

Lauren nodded. 'So, what you're saying is that I can go baby shopping as soon as I want?'

'Why not?'

She smiled. 'What sort of grandfather do you think you'll be?'

'A cool one, obviously. What about you? I

don't see you as one to sit and knit mittens or anything.'

'That's a stereotype!'

He laughed. 'Sorry!'

He gave her a friendly nudge with his elbow and she pushed him back and then they were both laughing and then he was holding her and pulling her close and suddenly she was breathless and staring up into his eyes.

And then they were kissing.

Something happened when she kissed Oliver. The world and its cares melted away. All her worries disappeared and all that mattered was the press of his lips on hers, his body against hers, and all she could think was, *More. More!* As if she wanted to consume him. As if she wanted all of him, her hunger for him insatiable.

Was it because he was available to her now, whereas before she had always had to share him, with the hospital, with his shifts, with his patients and with the girls. She'd never got Oliver one hundred percent to herself when they'd become parents. She'd always felt that part of his mind was elsewhere.

But now? Today? Since they'd been sleeping together again she felt as if he was hers again. One hundred percent hers, no sharing. His focus was totally on her and it was the most intoxicating drug she had ever experienced.

When the kiss broke apart and she was left breathing heavily, desiring more, she pressed her forehead against his and looked deeply into his eyes.

'Let's go home.'

Oliver nodded, his eyes dark with desire, and he took her hand and led her back to his car.

CHAPTER TWELVE

TODAY WAS THE DAY, the partial face transplant, and Lauren and Oliver had got to work extra early. She'd set her alarm for five a.m. and when it had gone off she'd woken with a start in Oliver's arms, reaching over to turn it off.

'Time for work.'

'I don't want to.' Oliver pulled her close. 'I'd rather stay here with you.'

Lauren had laughed as his lips had found her throat and begun to nuzzle. 'You'd rather stay here than perform one of the greatest surgeries a maxillofacial surgeon can do?'

'You're more fun.'

'Am I?'

Oliver could do amazing things with his lips and it was a struggle to not let herself succumb to his ministrations, but eventually he lifted his head and looked her in the eyes.

'Yes.'

'I don't believe you.' She'd laughed again and rolled away from him, out of his arms, and strode naked to her bathrobe, hanging on the back of the bedroom door. 'Come on. Shower.'

He'd sat up, propped on one elbow. 'Together?'

'If you're a good boy.'

He'd grinned and leapt naked from her bed.

The shower had taken a little longer than expected, but they'd got to work on time, as traffic was light. Oliver had headed on up to see Mina and make sure that she was being prepped and was getting her final bloods done, just as a precaution to make sure that her blood count was good and that she wasn't harbouring any infection before her big surgery, whereas Lauren had headed off to ready the donor, Anjuli.

Lauren's surgery would start at the same time as Oliver's, only in different theatres. As she assisted in removing the donor tissue, Oliver would be prepping Mina's face to receive it. It was going to be a long day. A difficult day. An exhausting day. But they were ready for it. So her mind was a little elsewhere as she got in the lift, not noticing who was already in there.

'Er...earth to Mum?'

Lauren looked up. 'Willow! Hello, darling.' She gave her daughter a hug. 'How are you? You're in early.'

'No, I'm still on night shift. I get to go home in an hour,' she said with a yawn.

'Long night?'

'Not too bad. I managed to grab a couple of hours.' Willow was looking at her strangely, eyes bright, looking slightly amused.

Lauren touched her face. 'Do I have toothpaste around my mouth or…?'

'No.'

'Then what is it?'

'Nothing!' Willow tried to look innocent, but she'd never been great at hiding her feelings.

'Come on, what is it?'

Her daughter laughed. 'It's just I heard a rumour, is all.'

'A rumour?'

There were plenty of rumours in a hospital. There always were. Right now, everyone was buzzing with the news about Dylan and Poppy.

'About you and Dad.'

Lauren swallowed, tried not to blush. 'About me and Oliver?' She tried to sound surprised. As if there could be nothing about them that was at all interesting.

Willow leaned in. 'Are you and Dad dating?'

'What?' Lauren tried to look shocked, appalled. 'Whatever makes anyone think that?'

Willow shrugged. 'You've been seen, apparently. Out and about together. And it's been noted that you leave together at night and arrive together in the morning and Dad is sometimes wearing what he wore the day before…'

'Ridiculous! We went out and celebrated *once*. When we got the news about Kayley's baby. That's all!' She tried not to flush with her lie to her daughter, but she didn't want Willow getting any ideas, or getting hopeful that her parents might be getting back together. She didn't want her kids involved. Right now, it was between her and Oliver and they were having fun, as they should have had before, and she didn't need the pressure of her daughter's expectations. Or anyone else's. 'You ought to try telling people to get their facts right.'

'Uh-huh. Then why did I see you come in with Dad this morning? I was on my break, not stalking you, and I saw you come in and you both looked...'

'What? Looked what?'

'Happy. Contented. You smiled at each other with a smile that said *I've recently seen you naked*,' Willow whispered as the doors to the lift pinged open on the floor Lauren needed.

She flushed with embarrassment and stepped out of the lift. 'You're seeing what you want to see.'

Willow held the lift door open. 'So, you're denying it?'

'Yes.'

'And Dad will say the same if I ask him?'

'Of course.'

'Hmm.' Willow smiled as if she didn't believe her and as the doors closed she heard her shout, 'Methinks thou doth protest too much!'

Lauren stared at the lift doors as they closed and it took their daughter away to another floor. She pulled her phone from her pocket and texted Oliver.

We have a problem.

Oliver was hours into the transplant surgery when the donor team arrived with the replacement facial tissue for Mina. Lauren brought it in and passed it over to his team, who prepped it, rinsing it before it was brought over to him for reattachment.

This was the difficult part. Each blood vessel needed reconnecting. Each nerve. The tissue had been checked for measurements so that it fitted Mina perfectly. It had taken years to find a donor who was the exact match for Mina, not just in blood typing, but in skin colour, size, age. And he and his team could stand here all day doing the reattachment, go through all of this process and still, at the end of the day, Mina's body might reject the tissue.

It was a risk. It was always a huge risk. But Mina had wanted to go ahead, to take that risk, and if she was willing to undergo it then they were willing to help her and make her feel better about herself every time she looked in a mirror.

But he was ready. They were all ready. They'd practised this. Hours and hours of practice so that the surgery ran smoothly, anticipating all the possible problems mid-surgery, but so far, it was going as well as could be expected. Mina had remained stable, her heart rate and blood pressure staying in normal ranges.

By rights, he should be exhausted, having stood here for so long, concentrating so hard, focused intensely, but he was far from tired. He was ecstatic, thrilled, adrenaline coursing through him with every stitch, with every cut.

He'd not felt that way just before he'd scrubbed. He'd received that text from Lauren that people were gossiping about them in the hospital, and that had thrown him slightly. But he hoped the news about Dylan Harper being the father of Poppy Evans' baby was juicier for everyone and that their relationship would not be as interesting.

Oliver glanced up and met Lauren's eyes. She wasn't at the forefront with the other surgeons. Her part was over now and she could only observe, but he knew exactly where she stood in his theatre. Of course he did. Ever since she'd come back to London, he'd known exactly where she was, sensing her every time. The way she looked back at him was encouraging.

You can do this. You're amazing.

And he smiled behind his mask as a particularly tricky part of the face with the trigeminal nerves came together. He was working with a brilliant plastics team, a world class ear, nose and throat team. His max fax crew and other reconstructive surgeons. There was a lot of training and a lot of egos in the room, but all of that had been pushed aside to focus on giving Mina the best chance of living life with a normal face, and not one ravaged by scars and burns.

As the final few stitches were put into place and he was able to relax, the effect of the adrenaline began to wane and he felt the exhaustion hit as he gazed up at the clock. They'd been there all day. An entire day! And not once had he thought of, or needed, food or water. It was amazing how surgery could make you feel, but he knew he would crash tonight and sleep well. He thought about crawling into bed with Lauren, holding her tight and snuggling into her and falling asleep in her arms.

It would be the perfect end to the perfect day.

They were out Christmas shopping the weekend after Mina's surgery. Lauren loved shopping for presents and this year she was looking for-

ward to it even more, because the presents she
bought for people today, she would actually get
to see them open. Because this time she lived
back home in London, where she belonged, and
didn't have to resort to making a video call with
her girls and blowing them kisses over a screen
and wishing them a Merry Christmas.

Oliver had offered to go with her and she'd
happily accepted. She and Oliver used to love
Christmas shopping. She recalled that very often
he wasn't available to go shopping with her when
the girls were young, but there'd been one or
two occasions when he had made it and they'd
always had the best time.

'Oh, let's go in here!' she said, steering him
towards a jewellery shop. Both their girls, Kayley and Willow, wore a charm bracelet, and
she wanted to buy them a charm each. It was a
tradition that she'd kept up for five years now,
ever since they'd both got them. Kayley liked
any type of charm, whereas Willow preferred
charms that were animals. She'd once joked that
her mum would create a zoo on her wrist by the
time she'd filled it up.

They perused the cabinets and displays, ooh-
ing and aahing over the various charms, and
eventually they found a perfect giraffe charm for
Willow, and for Kayley, because she was now

pregnant, they found one that looked like an old-fashioned pram.

'They're perfect!' she said as the sales girl wrapped it for them and handed them over with a smile.

'Where to next?' Oliver asked.

'Bookshop, of course!'

He laughed. 'Of course.'

No shopping trip was complete without going into a bookshop and they knew that Aaron loved reading spy thrillers and one had recently been released that Lauren had had her eye on for him.

'Do you think we should buy something for the baby?' she asked him as they browsed the shelves looking for it.

He thought for a moment. 'Might be fun to get a little something. But what?'

'Baby-gro?'

'Hmm. I was thinking of something bigger.'

She smiled. 'Like what?'

'The crib.'

'Really? Don't you think Kayley and Aaron would want to choose that? We have no idea how they're going to decorate the nursery.'

'Actually, Aaron told me that they're hoping to keep it quite neutral and modern.'

'But don't babies prefer bold colours and shapes?'

'I think so.'

'I think that's something we could get by going out with them, so they can give us their opinion. I don't want to step on anyone's toes. Ah, there it is!' Lauren found the book she was looking for and picked it up, turning it to the back to double-check the blurb.

'Then what about something practical, where colour doesn't matter so much? I was thinking the car seat. Safety first and all of that.'

Lauren nodded. 'That's a good idea. It can be quite an expense and it'll be nice to think that a gift we bought them will bring that baby safely home from the hospital. All right, let's do that!'

Oliver grinned. 'We can do a cute little pack of Baby-gros too, though.'

'Motherland next, then?'

He nodded. 'Motherland next.'

They had a whale of a time in Motherland. There were so many cute things that they wanted to buy, so many cute clothes! They bought a car seat, two packs of Baby-gros, some vests, new-born nappies and a mobile to hang over the cot, made of soft, neutral-coloured animals in shades of beige and mushroom and cream. Lauren saw a couple of cute cuddly toys that she wanted to buy and was about to pick up the ones she liked when she became aware of a vibration in her coat pocket. Her phone.

'Oh, hang on.' She delved into her pocket to

reach for it, but it stopped ringing by the time she got it out.

Missed call

She clicked on the phone symbol and frowned when she saw the name.

'Everything okay?' Oliver asked.

It was Mike from Edinburgh who'd tried to call her. Why, though? Why would he need to call her? They'd said everything they'd needed to say—they were no longer involved.

Lauren pushed the phone back in her pocket and forced a smile. She would not let Mike ruin this day. This day was perfect. Out Christmas shopping with Oliver again, enjoying this time with him. Walking around the shops, holding his hand, laughing together, shopping for their girls and their future grandchild. This was the kind of family activity she'd missed out on, being so far away in Edinburgh.

'Everything's fine. Cold caller,' she lied, hating that she was lying, but she didn't want Mike's name to ruin this bubble they were in. Their fun bubble.

Because, right now, neither of them had talked about what was happening between them. She'd even denied anything was happening to Willow when she'd heard that gossip on the hospital grapevine. She and Oliver didn't need other people ruining what they had right now and whilst they lived in the moment, whilst they didn't think too hard about what they were doing, then it was simply fun and she'd earned that, after all these years. Lauren was in a place where she was happy and coming back to London had been the right call.

'Okay. Oh, we must pop next door. I want to pick up a new tie for Dev.'

'Your registrar?'

'I buy him a new tie every year and he buys me one. We try to outdo each other with something ridiculous, it's become quite the tradition,' he said, laughing.

She gazed at her ex-husband. He truly had changed with time. He was more relaxed. He was happier than she'd ever seen him. He was secure in who he was now and she loved the way he looked at her, the way he made her feel. She hoped that she made him feel good too.

'Talking of tradition, what do you do for Christmas these days?'

He shrugged. 'Sometimes I've volunteered to work on Christmas Day. No biggie. Being in hospital on Christmas Day is so different to any other day. People are happier, more relaxed, as much as they can be, depending on their situation. The staff are cheerier. We look out for each other more.'

'And when you're not at the hospital, working?'

'I went to Kayley's last year. She did a big lunch for everyone.'

Oh, yes. Lauren remembered now. She'd done a video call with them and she remembered seeing Oliver just out of frame and feeling so incredibly jealous of him being with their girls, whilst she was stuck up in Edinburgh, working.

'And this year?'

'Willow's. She's offered. Are you coming?'

Lauren smiled. 'I am! Apparently, Kayley and Aaron will be there too, so it will be a real family Christmas for us all.'

'That's great.' Oliver looked really happy to hear that she was going to be there.

Was it possible that everything in her life was finally working out? Were the Shaw family about to have the best Christmas they had ever had? They'd all be together. Kayley was pregnant with their first grandchild. Lauren was secure at work and in her career. She and Oliver were finally being how they ought to have been a long time ago.

Her phone beeped. A text message.

She should have turned away. She should have positioned herself so Oliver couldn't see, but she didn't think about it. She had no reason to think about it. She'd not thought there would be anything to hide. But she pulled her phone from her pocket and looked at the screen. It was Mike again.

Call me. Mike x.

She slid her phone back in her pocket as quickly as she could, stomach rolling, unsure as to why Mike would be calling her and wanting her to call him back.

Lauren knew that Oliver had seen her screen, but he was pretending he hadn't. A frown was on his face, a frown he was trying to hide as he sorted through the cuddly toys, trying to find one that he liked.

Clearly, he thought this was none of his business any more.

They were just bed partners right now.

Neither of them had spoken of the future, or had stated what they were, or whether there were any rules.

Maybe she'd misread the whole thing and he wasn't as into her as she was into him.

'I don't know why he's texting me,' she said, needing to explain.

Oliver forced a smile. 'It's fine! None of my business, right?' But he didn't look fine. He looked annoyed. He looked wrong-footed. He looked…angry.

She couldn't believe a simple text could pierce their bubble so easily.

Maybe she and Oliver weren't as strong as she'd thought they were.

CHAPTER THIRTEEN

THIS MIKE GUY probably had a reason to text her, right? Maybe it was something to do with one of her patients back in Edinburgh. Maybe she'd left some stuff at his place.

Maybe he still has feelings for her and wants her to come back.

He'd tried to forget it, tried to ignore the text message, but it had tainted the rest of the Christmas shopping trip for him. Oliver had tried to be normal, to still be his usual relaxed, jovial self, but seeing that guy text Lauren, seeing his name come up on the screen, seeing that message.

Call me. Mike x

He'd put a kiss—what was that all about? He must still harbour feelings for Lauren. He had to. Lauren was great—amazing! Why wouldn't the guy want her back? Perhaps this Mike guy had realised what a mistake he'd made by going after other women and wanted back the one woman he couldn't have. Some guys were like that, wanted what was unavailable. It made them feel safe. Their treacherous little hearts wouldn't be in danger with someone who was unavailable, right?

The question was, did Lauren feel the same way? She'd acted as if she didn't understand why he'd texted, but she'd not been surprised by the text.

And then he remembered. There'd been a call, moments before. She'd said it was a cold call, but her expression had said something else.

Was Mike calling her regularly? Were they talking? Maybe this wasn't even his first contact—maybe they'd been talking all the time she'd been down here in London.

Had Lauren rebounded from Mike and into Oliver's arms? And, like a fool, he'd let her in. He'd told her he was free of Daria—she'd told him she was free of Mike, but she'd only just broken up with him. What if she still had feelings for Mike and she was playing them both?

Oliver groaned. He hated feeling this way, and he hated more than anything realising that he was capable of thinking that Lauren would do that to him. She wasn't that kind of woman, never had been. Why would she be now? She'd not changed. She was decent and caring and loving. She would not play off two guys to keep her options open.

There had to be another explanation. He had to believe that this was about one of her old patients. Perhaps they had a message for her? Or perhaps this Mike had an update he wanted to pass on? They did that when they met patients socially and they asked to be remembered to their surgeon. He had to believe it was that and not some other thing.

Did he have any right to tell Lauren that she must be honest with him? Did he have the right to demand the truth?

Could he be honest with himself and admit that he was jealous? And if he was jealous—which it seemed pretty obvious that he was—then he had to also admit to himself that Lauren had come to mean a huge amount to him again. He'd always love her, but was he in love with her again?

It was an answer he would have to find, or he would drive himself insane.

Kayley looked up from her desk in her office, then laughed. 'What on earth is that?'

'A bauble for your tree.'

'It's a pair of bootees. Baby bootees.'

'Yes, it is. I wanted to get one that said *Baby's*

first Christmas, but your dad said that technically it wouldn't be that until next year.'

Kayley came from around her desk, kissed Lauren on the cheek and took the bauble. 'Dad's right.'

'Well, don't tell him that. We don't want to set a precedent.' Lauren laughed and looked about her daughter's office. She'd never been to Kayley's place of work before, but it seemed nice—modern and lively. Kayley had a corner office, with a view of London from the window on her right.

'Where is he? Work?'

Lauren nodded, trying to smile but feeling nervous. She'd come here with an agenda. Kayley was the only one she could ask, the only one she could confide in, because Willow was a doctor and worked at the same place as she and Oliver, so she'd be biased.

'What's up? You look strange.'

'I need to talk to you. I need advice and you're quite analytical and I think that you will be honest with me.'

'Okay. This sounds like it's going to need tea.' She pressed a button on her intercom. 'Sandra, can you bring in a pot of tea for two, please? Oh, and those little biscuits we had yesterday.'

'Cravings?' Lauren asked, trying to lighten the mood.

'Yes. Incredibly so. Baby seems to want all the junk food. Biscuits, sweets, cakes, chocolate, you name it—if it's going to raise my cholesterol, baby wants it.'

Lauren smiled as she continued to look around the room. A neat little cactus in a pot. A framed picture of Kayley and Aaron in Croatia. A bookshelf full of law texts. A filing cabinet. A computer.

'Sit down, Mum. You're making me feel anxious.'

'Oh. Sorry.' She slid into a seat opposite her daughter's desk and began to twiddle her thumbs.

'So…what is it?'

'Don't you want to wait for the tea and biscuits?'

'No, I want you to tell me why you've crossed half of London in your lunch break to come and see me. Oh, God, is Dad sick?' She leaned forward, a panicked look on her face.

'No, no! Lord, no! Nothing like that. No, I just want your considered opinion on something. On a choice.'

'A choice?'

There was a slight knock at the door and then in came Sandra with a tray. She laid it on the table and disappeared again, closing the door behind her.

'What choice, Mum?'

'On whether I should stay here or go back to Edinburgh.'

Kayley stared. And blinked.

Mina was doing very well, healing nicely, with no infection and no sign of rejection. Oliver had been staying at the hospital to watch her and his other patients around the clock, ever since his shopping trip with Lauren. Keeping busy kept his mind off all the visions he had of Lauren being touched by another man.

He knew he was being irrational and illogical and that all he needed to do to clear this up was to talk to Lauren, but he was so afraid of what he was going to hear that he didn't. He kept their conversations when she rang him fun and light and upbeat. He tried to make it clear that he had no claim on her, no expectations.

They'd even had one night at the cinema to see a film, but he'd not been able to concentrate on it at all. When they'd got back outside in the falling snow, Lauren had started talking about a particular scene in the film and he'd had no earthly idea what she was going on about. And then, when she'd snuggled into him for warmth, he'd closed his eyes in rapture, wondering if this was the last time he'd get to hold her like this. And if it was, then he needed to truly appreciate it and remember every moment. He couldn't believe he was about to lose the love of his life to that lowlife rapscallion who had already cheated on her.

He was just on his way to Theatre to operate on a patient when Lauren caught up with him in the corridor. 'Hey, are you free? Can we talk?'

His stomach plummeted. She wanted to talk? This couldn't be good. 'I'm on my way to a surgery.'

'The rhinoplasty on the Treacher Collins patient?'

Treacher Collins was a rare genetic disorder that could affect the way a patient's face developed. It could affect ears, cheekbones, eyes and the jaw, causing many problems, both physically and sometimes socially.

He nodded.

'So you'll be done in about two to three hours?'

'Yes, but then I've got other patients and—'

'I really need to talk to you, Oliver. It's important.'

He sighed and checked the time. He might be done by one o'clock. 'I suppose I could meet you in the canteen. About one?'

'One o'clock? You're sure?'

Wow. She really wanted to peg him into a time. Must be serious.

I don't want serious. I don't want the serious conversation where you tell me you're going back to that creep.

'If the surgery overruns, I'll get a message to you.'

'Thank you.'

He walked away then, not trusting himself to stay and say anything else.

Was she really going to walk away from them all again?

Lauren sat with a coffee in front of her, but it had been cooling for a while.

Oliver was late. Maybe his surgery had overrun. But he'd told her he would get a message to her and she'd not received anything so...

Things hadn't been quite right since Mike had got back in touch. She'd sensed a change in him and knew that he'd seen the text arrive and who it was from and though he'd pretended to be the same, he wasn't. There'd been a distance between them and perhaps that was his way of preparing himself for her to leave.

But she wasn't going to do that. She couldn't, could she? Her life was here now. She wanted to be here. Kayley was going to have her first child in a few months and work was great here. She liked the hospital, she liked the staff and she loved being back with Oliver.

Only…she couldn't help but linger over Mike's suggestion about her going back. It would be an amazing opportunity and would really put her name as a reconstructive surgeon on the map. She wanted to be the best. She wanted to be like Oliver and have people come from all over to be operated on by her.

She'd spoken to the girls, but now she wanted to talk to Oliver. Get it out in the open. Let him know what had been said and what she'd decided. Or thought she'd decided.

What if you're doing the wrong thing?

In the distance, she saw Oliver enter the canteen and she sat up straighter and raised a hand to grab his attention. He headed on over to her, his expression impassive, almost stony, as he slid into the seat opposite.

Where was his jolly Christmas mood of only a few days ago? Where was the happy, laughing Oliver who'd kept dragging her back into bed every time she'd got up to try and get dressed?

'I don't have long,' he said.

'Nor me. But I thought we ought to talk.'

'If you're leaving us, then just say it.'

Us. Not me.

'Mike called. As you *know*. He wanted me to get in touch because he had an offer for me.'

'Oh? What kind of offer?'

'There's an opportunity for me to return to

Edinburgh and work with Mike and his team on bringing over a group of people from India that have suffered burns and bodily disfigurements. It's going to be a big promo thing for the Great Northern and it's going to be a yearly programme. He wants a good team around him and he's asked me to join him on a permanent basis. Better pay. Better hours. So, yeah. They want me to go back.'

She watched him mull over this news, his expression getting stonier, his frown deepening.

'And are you going to go?'

'It's a great opportunity for me. It would be a step up in my career, look great on my CV. And I'd be doing important work on people who need it and can't receive the treatment they need where they are.' She wanted him to see that she understood what a career opportunity this was for her.

'I see.'

'Only I've needed to think about it, obviously. I didn't want to make a knee-jerk reaction, especially as I've really settled here and begun to know everyone.'

He nodded.

'And then there's you and the girls. The baby. I want to be here for that, but what if I don't get an opportunity like this again? I mean, is the Great Southern about to have a programme like this?'

'Not that I know of.'

'Exactly. I'm torn.'

'But you said you've settled here. You said you came back to be with family, that you felt alone up north. Why would you want to go back to that?'

'Because it's not just about feelings, is it? I have a chance here at becoming a great surgeon.'

'You are a great surgeon. You took part in a partial face transplant just weeks into your time here. Without you, that donor tissue wouldn't have been as perfect as it was. And you want to be here! You want to be here for all of us. For Willow. Kayley. Me. The *baby*. We're all getting used to having you back again and it's been wonderful.'

'Thank you. I appreciate that. But if I stay, will I *regret* prioritising my family over my career again if I don't take it? Because I did that once, remember? I let you go on ahead and chase your dreams and I stayed behind to be a mum. I raised my babies, I put my career on hold for decades, because I put them first. Yet I'm just getting started with my career again and I want to be the best, Oliver, the very best! If I let this opportunity go, I may just regret it.'

Oliver shook his head, anger crossing his face as he stood up, clearly fuming. 'And is that all?'

'What do you mean?'

'You're sure all this talk about going back is just a career opportunity?'

'I don't understand.'

'This Mike…this hotshot reconstructive guy who, I might remind you, has not proven reliable or loyal to you in the past, suddenly wants you back? As just a surgeon?'

'What are you implying?' She did not like what he was suggesting. Was he trying to imply that Mike wanted her back for other reasons? 'You think he wants to add me back into his harem, is that it? You think I'd go back for that?'

'I don't know what to think!' Oliver's voice was raised now, everyone looking at them, then pretending not to.

'Oliver!'

He leaned in, angry. 'You said you were settling here. You said you were happy here. You said you were looking forward to being back with your family and how you were going to spoil that new grandchild we're about to have. And what have *we* been doing, huh? Just messing around? Just having fun? Was I *convenient* to you? Were you using me until you got a better offer?'

She stared at him in shock. 'No! Of course not! I can't believe you're acting this way. Kayley and Willow both think that this would be a good chance for me to further my career—'

'*The girls?* You've spoken to them already about this? Before talking to me?'

Never before had she seen him this angry. Not even when they'd decided on divorcing. But now he seemed apoplectic with rage as he stormed away and she was left alone, on the verge of tears, staring after his retreating form.

Lauren sank back into her seat and dabbed at her eyes with a napkin, trying not to lock gazes with anyone else in the canteen. Her heart was thudding painfully in her chest. From embarrassment, from shame, from anger and from grief.

She'd not meant to hurt him. She'd not thought he would get this upset. She'd honestly believed that he would sit and listen to her and calmly go over her options with her.

Maybe they'd not been having fun, after all.

Maybe it had been so much more than that.

CHAPTER FOURTEEN

OLIVER KNEW HE had no right to be angry with Lauren but he couldn't explain how he felt, not even to himself. Feeling that he was the last to find out, when he was the one who stood to lose the most if she left him again.

It was now a week before Christmas and he'd hoped so much to have a Christmas to remember, with Lauren back by his side. He'd pictured it. It would have been perfect. Waking up in her bed, going over to Willow's and helping cook dinner together, pulling crackers, telling stupid jokes, being together as a family and then at bedtime, holding her close and telling her that she was the best Christmas present he could ever receive.

She was back and their relationship had seemed better than it ever was.

Had. Past tense.

Of course he could see why she might consider going back to Edinburgh. It was an amazing career opportunity for her. It was the sort of programme he wished the Great Southern was doing too, something he'd leap at for the lives they could change, for the people they could make better and improve their quality of life. Of course she should consider it and of course she was right. She had put her family before her career once before and her time was now. He was where he was today because of her career sacrifice to stay at home and raise their girls and give them the lives that they deserved.

Had he ever truly thanked her for that? Had he ever gone out of his way to make her feel special and appreciated? Or had he been working so hard, grafting every single day, sacrificing holidays and birthdays and yes, Christmases, that he'd just taken her sacrifice for granted?

Was he going to make her stay and hold her back again?

He hated himself for making her feel that way, that he was putting this pressure on her. But if he took that pressure off, if he saw her, apologised, then he'd lose her again, lose what they had, and he wasn't sure he could be the orchestrator of that either.

'Damn it!' His stitch slipped and he had to retie it before going onto the next. He was doing a lower eyelid reconstruction on a patient who had lost a large part of tissue there, due to a basal cell carcinoma, having taken some skin from the forearm to replace it.

'You okay?' Dev, his registrar, looked at him over his facemask.

No. No, he wasn't okay. He couldn't think straight and this patient had been through enough and needed someone who was truly focused on the task at hand.

'Just a lot on my mind. Do you want to finish for me? I'll stay and observe.'

'You're sure? Thanks, boss.'

He stood and watched Dev attach the new flap of skin, making sure they reconstructed the tissue near the tear ducts accurately, so that there wouldn't be so much swelling there afterwards that might block them. They didn't want to get an infection in there. Dev worked well. He was a good registrar and had picked up a lot of good habits from watching Oliver at work.

'You're a family man, Dev.'

Dev raised an eyebrow. 'Er, yeah, I've got a big family.'

'They'd miss you if you weren't around at Christmas, right?'

'Of course!'

'But if you'd been offered an unmissable career opportunity and it meant you had to leave totally—move house, uproot everything—would they mind?'

'They'd miss me, but I think they'd understand. Why? Are you about to offer me something?'

Oliver shook his head. 'Just thinking about something, is all.'

'Are you leaving us? I'm not sure I'd be happy about losing my mentor.'

'Not me either.'

'Ah.'

'*Ah?* What does *ah* mean?'

'It's Lauren, isn't it?'

He sighed. Was he so obvious? But he nodded.

'And you guys are close again? I try not to listen to gossip, but even I've seen how happy you've been this last month or so with her here.'

'Her ex contacted her about this job offer back in Edinburgh and she's considering it.'

'Right. Gotcha.' Dev tied off the last stitch and dabbed at the area with a pad. 'Well, you know what they say?'

'What's that?'

'If you love someone, set them free.'

'That's an idiotic saying! Why would you let them go?'

'So you love her, then?'

Oliver stared at Dev. He'd only meant to share the hypothetical and yet here he was, being asked out loud by a colleague if he was back in love with his ex-wife!

'Sorry. Not my business. Forget I asked anything.'

'I do love her, I always have, and she sacrificed her career for me once before. Can I really ask her to do that again?'

'Can I speak candidly?'

'Of course.'

'If you stop her from going then she may resent you for the rest of her life and that will eventually break up anything you share right now.'

'I'm not sure we share anything right now.'

'You're wrong. You're both hurting and you both need to talk to one another.'

'But every time I look at her, I just want to pull her close and never let her go.'

Dev nodded. 'Then you, my friend, are in a quandary.'

'Thanks.'

His registrar pulled off his gown and gloves. 'For what it's worth, I think you two are great and, selfishly, I hope she stays because since she's been back you've let me do more procedures than I've ever got to do before!' He winked as he headed into the scrub room.

Oliver smiled and pulled off his own gown and gloves and mask. As he scrubbed, he became aware of his mobile phone ringing again and again. It would have to wait. Whoever it was would have to wait. When he picked up his phone, he saw that Lauren had tried to call him three separate times.

What did she want? To tell him that she'd made a decision? That she was leaving because her ex-husband had behaved terribly?

He was in no rush to hear that. So he silenced his phone and went to check on a patient.

CHAPTER FIFTEEN

WHERE WAS HE? Why wasn't he answering his phone?

Lauren thrust her phone back into her pocket as the taxi driver pulled up in front of the hospital and she found a note to pay him with. She wasn't even aware of what kind of note she thrust at him and told him to keep the change as she leapt from the vehicle and ran towards A&E.

She'd been sitting at home, staring at the wall, mulling over her decision to stay or to go, when the phone had rung and Willow, distraught on the other end, had informed her that Kayley and Aaron had been involved in a road traffic accident, a bad one, and all that she knew was that her sister and Aaron had been rushed to A&E.

She'd not been to A&E here before, so she wasn't aware of the layout as her gaze scanned the reception area, looking for the desk. There was a queue of people standing, waiting to be seen, the guy at the front holding a bloodied tea towel up against the side of his head.

It would take ages to ask, to stand there and queue and politely take her turn, and she couldn't bear to do that, so she rushed past them all, through the packed waiting room of the walking wounded and into Minors, looking for the sign that said Majors. Or Resus.

A nurse came out of a cubicle, sliding the curtain behind her closed, and noticed the distraught look on Lauren's face. 'Are you okay?'

'I'm looking for my daughter, Kayley Smith. She was brought in by ambulance with her husband, Aaron. They've been in a car accident.'

'All right, come with me. I'll take you to the family room whilst I go and find out what's happening, okay?'

Lauren nodded, even though she didn't want to be in a family room. She wanted to be by her daughter's side, holding her hand, telling her everything would be all right, whilst she fired questions at the doctors treating her.

But when the nurse opened the family room door she saw Willow inside, crying.

'Willow!' She rushed into her younger daughter's arms. 'Oh, my love.' She held Willow tightly, desperate to ask her if she knew any more, but staying silent because she knew how much her daughter needed to be held right now, rather than questioned.

Eventually, they broke apart and settled down onto the sofa. 'Tell me what you know.'

'A doctor has just been in. She's sustained a head injury and she's unconscious.'

A head injury? Lauren's heart sank. That could be anything, from minor to major. It could just be concussion, or shock, or low blood pressure. But, equally, it could also be a fractured skull, or a brain bleed, or worse.

'And she's bleeding. She could be losing the baby!'

'Oh, my God!' Lauren pulled Willow close, not willing to think about that. After all that Kayley and Aaron had been through, trying to get pregnant, if she woke and found out she'd lost that precious baby...

If she even wakes up at all.

Lauren wanted to throw up. She felt so helpless.

'Is your father here yet?'

Willow shook her head. 'I called you and you said you'd call him.'

'He's not picking up. I think he might be avoiding my calls—we've had a little falling-out.' She felt embarrassed to say it. Their argument seemed so insignificant in the light of the news about her daughter and son-in-law. 'Can you try him?'

Willow nodded.

'What have they said about Aaron?'

'Minor injuries. Cuts and scrapes. He's being stitched up.'

She nodded, listening as Willow called her dad.

He picked up and in the quiet of the room she heard him say, 'Hi, pumpkin!'

Oliver said nothing else she could hear as Willow told him the news and then ended the call.

Willow looked pale and shocked as she glanced at her mum with her tear-stained face and said quietly, 'He's on his way.'

They sat around Kayley's bed in a dread silence, each of them shocked by the visage of their loved one lying in a bed in a now medically induced coma.

Oliver stood by the foot of the bed, whereas Aaron and Lauren sat either side, each of them holding one of Kayley's hands.

'It was a drunk driver,' Aaron said. 'On his way to a work Christmas party, the police said.'

Oliver closed his eyes in dismay. Too many people still thought that they were safe to drive when they'd been drinking and threw all the rules out of the window, just because it was Christmas. They always thought they were sober enough to drive. They always thought they'd get away with it.

'Was he, or she, hurt?'

'Minor injuries. Why do bad people always seem to get away with things like this, whereas good people, lovely people, my beautiful, pregnant wife, have to suffer for *their* bad choices?'

Aaron was angry, but so was Oliver. They all were. That things like this were still allowed to happen... For a long time, with the advent of electric cars, Oliver had often said that cars shouldn't be able to start unless the driver took a breath test that was somehow registered by the vehicle. Surely the technology existed.

He'd said it to Willow earlier, and she'd agreed, but said, *'People would just get their friends to breathe into the breathalyser for them.'*

Perhaps she was right.

'I'm going to get a coffee. Or what passes for coffee in this place. Can I get anyone anything?' Aaron asked.

They'd been sitting by Kayley's bedside for well over twenty-four hours.

'I'll come with you,' Willow said. 'I need to stretch my legs.'

Aaron stood, turned to Oliver. 'You'll call if anything changes?'

'Of course.' He gave Aaron a hug and squeezed him tight, knowing how he must feel to see his pregnant wife lying unconscious in a hospital bed, with tubes and on a ventilator. If that had ever been Lauren… He sat opposite her now after Aaron and Willow left and took his daughter's hand. It was warm but unresponsive and he felt tears prick at the backs of his eyes.

'I'm sorry, Oliver.' Lauren spoke, looking across at him.

He met her gaze, heart breaking. 'I'm sorry too. All our issues seem stupid in comparison to this, so… I'm sorry I reacted badly. That I got angry, that I shouted at you in public. That was wrong of me and you should take that job, the one in Edinburgh. When this is all over and Kayley's better, you should go. Fly. Be brilliant in Edinburgh. I'll be so proud of you.'

Lauren's gaze softened. 'Thank you. But I need to say sorry too. I should never have sprung the news about the job on you like that. I should have told you first. I never thought about how it might hurt you.'

'Call Mike. Accept the job. We're a family and families support one another.' He lifted his daughter's hand and kissed the back of it. 'Family is what matters and you give family what they need, and you need this. I should never have tried to hold you back.'

Lauren smiled at him. A soft smile. An appreciative smile. One of gratitude and thanks. 'I'm still deciding. And what with this now…'

'She'll get through this. Kayley's strong. So's the baby. We'll all be okay if you decide to go.'

He couldn't quite believe he was saying it, but maybe Dev was right. If you loved someone you had to let them go, and he loved Lauren. Deeply. Intensely. And he would rather see her walk away, knowing that she loved him for it, than she stayed and hated or resented him instead.

Poppy Evans had given birth to a baby girl. It was Christmas Eve and Lauren and Oliver were shaking Dylan's hand, congratulating him, glad for him.

'Her name's Belle and she's beautiful.'

'We're so happy for you, Dylan,' Oliver said.

'I forgot to ask. Any news on Kayley? And the baby?'

'The baby's fine, but they're going to try and wake Kayley today. The swelling in her brain has gone down, her intercranial pressure has normalised. They think it's the right time.'

'Let me know how it goes.' Dylan gave them both a quick hug. 'Gotta go. Take care, guys, and all the best.'

'Thanks.'

'Thank you.' Lauren and Oliver headed towards Kayley's room. She'd been put on a neurological ward and they had to get the lift to that floor, but they were both nervous about the out-come of the day. Would Kayley have any deficits? The neuro team didn't think so, but the brain was a mysterious organ still and no doctor could one hundred percent say whether she would be totally fine or not.

'Everything's going to be fine. Everything's going to go well,' Oliver muttered.

'We don't know that,' she said evenly, not wanting to get her hopes up.

'We have to believe that it will. It's Christmas. Good things happen at Christmas.'

'It's only Christmas Eve.'

'Christmas Eve and it's snowing outside. When has it last snowed at Christmas? I tell you, it's a time for miracles.'

As they walked down the corridor towards their daughter's room they saw Willow come out of it, crying, dabbing at her eyes and nose with a handkerchief.

'Willow! What's happened?' They rushed towards her and she couldn't speak, just pointed at Kayley's room.

Lauren rushed forward, bursting through the door to see her daughter lying in bed, eyes open, smiling and squeezing the hand of Aaron, who was crying happy tears. 'Kayley!'

They were all crying, all emotional, happily reassuring her that her baby was safe and doing well. She'd bled from her cervix, which had torn slightly in the accident, but the baby's heartbeat was strong and healthy.

'What do you remember of that night?' Lauren asked.

'Not much, thankfully.' Kayley smiled. 'The last thing I remember is Willow telling me that you guys were secretly getting it on.'

Lauren laughed and glanced, red-faced, at Oliver.

'I hope it's true. I hope you're together.' Kayley dozed off then—which was normal, the nurse who'd come into the room at their frantic button-pushing said.

Lauren found herself watching Oliver as they sat around Kayley's bed. Her family were going to be all right. They were all going to be all right. They'd got their Christmas miracle, but was there room for one more? One more miracle that would get her out of this terrible decision she'd been left with?

There was an uncertain future ahead of her and she needed to decide soon. Mike had been calling, anxious for her decision.

But she knew she needed to talk to Oliver.

CHAPTER SIXTEEN

'I THOUGHT I'D find you here.'

Snow was falling heavily on Hanover Square, delighting the ice-skaters whizzing around on the ice to festive music.

It seemed an age since they'd been here. In reality, it hadn't been that long and yet so much had happened in the meantime.

Oliver turned around and smiled at her. 'I was just thinking.'

'About?' She joined him at the rail and watched the skaters.

'About whether that triple axel was a pipe dream.'

He turned to her and she laughed, expecting something more serious to come out of his mouth. Once again, he had surprised her. Just like he'd surprised her at Kayley's bedside when he'd asked her to meet him here.

'Maybe if you practice?' she suggested, feeling the nerves in her tummy swell as she thought of what she had to ask him. Of what she wanted to say with all of her heart.

'I don't think so. Getting on the ice will only ever remind me of you.'

She looked at him then. Turned fully. Hesitated. The words were there, waiting to be said, but, once said, she would never be able to take them back. They'd be out there and she'd either be devastated or overjoyed. She truly did not know which.

'Oliver…can we talk?'

'Sure.' He led them away from the rink and over to a snow-covered bench. Behind them rose a giant Christmas tree that glinted and twinkled with lights as Oliver cleared the bench of snow so they could sit down. 'Though I'm not sure I'm ready for whatever you have to say.'

She smiled sadly. Nervously. 'Nor me.'

'Just say it.'

'Do it fast?'

'Rip off that plaster.'

Lauren liked the analogy. Sometimes it was best to do things quickly when you were afraid.

'I've been thinking a lot just lately and I've decided that I'm *not* going to take the job in Edinburgh.'

Oliver let out a breath, as if he'd been punched in the gut. 'You're not?'

'No.'

Why did he look so glum? She thought he'd be overjoyed. It made her faith waver.

'It's my fault, isn't it? I've forced you into staying. Ignore me, Lauren. I'll be okay. You should go if it's what you want.'

'But it's not what *I* want,' she implored. 'I want something else.'

He frowned. 'What is it? Anything. I'll give it to you, if it's within my power.'

She sucked in a breath, those nerves making her feel sick. 'I'm not the same person I was before, Oliver. I'm older. Wiser?' She laughed. 'I have my career here. It can be built here. My family is here. *You're* here.'

He reached for her gloved hands.

'I want to stay with those that I love, and that includes you. I'm in love with you, I've always been in love with you, but I need you to be honest with me right now and you need to tell me if you don't want to try again. But I do. I think we could work now if we make a solid attempt at it. And I mean more than the sex. More than the ice-skating and the skiing and the dinners and the snowman-making. I want to wake up with you every day. Go to sleep with you every night. I want us to be exclusive and I want you to be mine again. But even if you don't want *me*… I'm staying, so you'll just have to get used to seeing me around the place.'

She gave a nervous laugh then, unable to read his face. She used to be able to read him like a book but, like her, he'd changed. Time had done that to both of them.

He lifted her hands to his lips and kissed them. 'You're sure? You're saying all of this because you mean it? Because I'd hate to hold you back. I don't want you to resent me, not again.'

'This is my decision and only my decision. I have nothing to prove to anyone. I'm already a good reconstructive surgeon. This is a good programme and I can learn from the best here, but that's only a small consideration. The majority of my decision is because my heart is here. With Willow, with Kayley, with that baby yet to be born, but mostly it's here because of you. I love you, Oliver Shaw, and if you love me too then maybe one day we can come back and you could try that triple axel.'

He laughed, his head thrown back, exposing his throat, and then pulled her towards him for a kiss. When they broke apart, breathless and giddy, he looked deeply into her eyes. 'I love you, Lauren Shaw. Will you go out with me?'

Lauren nodded, smiling widely. 'I will. For ever and ever.'

And he kissed her again.

EPILOGUE

Two years later

'PRESENT TIME!'

Oliver called for them all to gather in the living area of the large London flat that he and Lauren had bought together. They'd been able to afford something really nice, spacious and modern and close enough to the hospital so that commuting hadn't become a chore.

Lauren sat by the Christmas tree with Kayley at her side and grandson Zachary being bounced up and down on her knee, giggling with glee. Aaron sat opposite, next to Willow's fiancé, and Willow herself sat cross-legged on the floor.

'Finally, Dad! Come on, old man!' Willow joked, pushing out the pouffe for him to sit on, so they could all be in a nice little circle.

He began to distribute the gifts—pyjama sets, fluffy socks, make-up for the girls, tickets to see shows in the West End, which Kayley and Willow were thrilled with. Aaron got a football kit of his favourite team and Oliver received some books he'd had on his wish list, with some chocolates and a fine bottle of single malt Scotch.

'There is one last present that I didn't put under the tree, that I wanted to give Lauren in front of everyone,' he said, smiling, feeling nervous, though he was pretty sure what she was going to say.

Their relationship over the last two years had been nothing short of wonderful, but they'd both agreed to not rush into marriage again. Not whilst Lauren was still occasionally going up to Edinburgh by train to consult—a situation that Oliver had encouraged her to do. Why not have everything, the best of both worlds? This way, Lauren got more exposure, more experience plus everything that she wanted here at home, and though he missed her when she'd disappear for a day or two, he always looked forward to her coming back.

Absence certainly made their hearts grow fonder.

But now all that was over he felt the time was right and he'd been thinking about this for a while. He'd consulted with the girls, got their opinions on a stone and shape, carat and cut, and now was the time.

Oliver got down on one knee and pulled a small ring box from his pocket.

Lauren gasped, hands covering her mouth.

'Lauren…you are my world, my everything, and you have made me the happiest man in existence ever since you arrived in my life. I love you so much, Baby Bird, and will you do me the honour of becoming my wife? Again.'

He proffered the box, opening it to reveal a perfect platinum diamond engagement ring.

'Oh, my goodness! Yes! Of course, yes!'

He stood with her and slid it onto her finger, kissing her and hugging her as everyone got to their feet to congratulate them.

Lauren examined the ring on her finger. 'It's beautiful! It's perfect!' She looked up at him. 'As are you.'

'Get a room!' Willow catcalled, making them all laugh.

He couldn't quite believe he was engaged to be married to her once again. But this time he knew with absolute certainty that they'd get it right.

Because time and life had given them both a second chance.

* * * * *

Look out for the next story in the
Christmas North and South quartet
Melting Dr. Grumpy's Frozen Heart
by Scarlet Wilson

And if you enjoyed this story,
check out these other great reads
from Louisa Heaton

Finding Forever with the Firefighter
Single Mom's Alaskan Adventure
Bound by Their Pregnancy Surprise

All available now!